FRANK COLLYMORE was at the heart of the West Indian literary renaissance in the 1940s and 50s, principally as publisher and editor of the magazine *Bim*. Through the magazine, he encouraged many promising young writers, with much the same generosity and enthusiasm as he influenced generations of boys at Combermere grammar school. Born in St Michael, Barbados, in 1893, he had attended the school himself from 1903 to 1910; he then taught at Combermere – mainly English and French – for the next fifty years. Some of his pupils were to become well-known West Indian writers, most notably George Lamming.

While devoted to teaching and editing, Collymore's diverse talents also embraced poetry, short-story writing, lexicography (he published notes on Barbadian dialect), painting, acting and broadcasting. While his poems have been published in several collections, his short stories are collected in this volume for the first time.

Collymore, who had been awarded the OBE in 1958, died in 1980, acknowledged as a major contributor to the cultural life of Barbados and the West Indies.

Harold Barratt is Professor of English at University College of Cape Breton, Nova Scotia, Canada; his teaching specialities include both Commonwealth literature, especially that of the West Indies, short fiction, and Shakespeare.

Reinhard Sander, Associate Professor of Black Studies and English, teaches African, African-American and Caribbean literature at Amherst College, USA.

FRANK COLLYMORE

THE MAN WHO LOVED ATTENDING FUNERALS AND OTHER STORIES

Edited by Harold Barratt and Reinhard Sander

HEINEMANN

Heinemann International Literature and Textbooks
A division of Heinemann Educational Books Ltd
Halley Court, Jordan Hall, Oxford OX2 8EJ

Heinemann: A Division of Reed Publishing (USA) Inc,
361 Hanover Street, Portsmouth, New Hampshire, 03801-3912, USA

Heinemann Educational Books (Nigeria) Ltd
PMB 5205, Ibadan
Heinemann Educational Boleswa
PO Box 10103, Village Post Office, Gaborone, Botswana

LONDON EDINBURGH PARIS MADRID
ATHENS BOLOGNA MELBOURNE SYDNEY
AUCKLAND SINGAPORE TOKYO

First published by Heinemann International Literature and Textbooks in 1993

Series Editor: Adewale Maja-Pearce

British Library Cataloguing in Publication Data
A catalogue record for this book is available from the British Library.

ISBN 0435 989316

Phototypeset by Cambridge Composing (UK) Ltd, Cambridge
Printed and bound in Great Britain
by Cox and Wyman Ltd, Reading, Berkshire

93 94 95 96 10 9 8 7 6 5 4 3 2 1

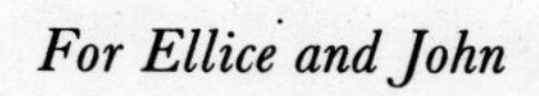

For Ellice and John

Contents

Foreword

It was inevitable that, given the range of his talents and output – acting, poetry, painting, editing, lexicography and schoolmastering – some aspect of Frank Collymore's contribution to the development of West Indian literature would find itself unattended and unexplored by scholars and critics. It is his short stories that have suffered, and it is therefore well and fitting that Professors Barratt and Sander have now drawn attention to this neglected product of a busy and fertile creative impulse.

Once, when asked which of his activities he enjoyed most and would wish, if he could, to concentrate on to the exclusion of all else, Frank Collymore replied unhesitatingly, 'Acting, of course!' The reply was a clue, not so much to any particular quality in his stage performances, as it was an indicator of what made him express himself in the variety of ways he chose.

If we were to judge his personality from his poetry, from the editorial entries in his notes on the Barbadian dialect, and, more especially, from his Collybeast drawings, we would conclude a mind given to whimsy and an eye for the comic side of human behaviour. If those findings are surprised by a macabre quality in some of the stories – what Professor Barratt has identified as 'the dark underside of the human mind' – then this collection of Frank Collymore's prose work leads us to see that fiction is often a repository of truth that might lie hidden but for the excavation work of scholars.

A new generation of readers of West Indian literature will find Professor Barratt's Afterword a valuable discussion of Frank Collymore's stories.

John Wickham

Foreword

[illegible]

Acknowledgements

We would like to express our deepest gratitude to Ellice Collymore for giving us permission to collect and edit her late husband's short fiction; John Wickham for his continuing encouragement and support; Paul Rockwell of Amherst College for introducing us to the mysteries and possibilities of an optical text scanner; and Dermot Quinn, Ellen Olmstead and Nuhad Jamal for their help with proofreading. Harold Barratt gratefully acknowledges the University College of Cape Breton's CERP Research Grant which facilitated his study of Frank Collymore's fiction.

The Editors

Proof

The telephone bell rang again, stridently, urgently.

Beside little Sonya's cot, Tamara, one hand continuing to stroke her sleeping daughter's head automatically, crouched scarcely breathing. She was afraid, afraid of the bell, afraid of the danger lurking out in the city, afraid of she scarcely knew what. Alone in the little flat without Gregor, she lived in constant fear of the terror that lay in wait in the darkness, waiting, watching . . . No one ever telephoned her. To Gregor the telephone was a business necessity. But all who knew Gregor knew that he was never at home at this hour, after dark. For then he would be at the newspaper office where he worked night after night from dusk till dawn. Perhaps it was a mistake . . . perhaps . . . no, there it went again . . . ting-a-ling, ting-a-ling! Her heart beat faster. Stay, though, perhaps it might be Gregor himself! Yet she was sure it wasn't Gregor. No, if it was, she would feel, she would know. She would not crouch there, paralysed almost, with memories, ugh, what memories, crowding out of the terrible past to choke her. Again! Mustering up such courage as she could command, she rose from beside the cot and crossed the room with short hesitating steps. She entered the adjoining room, the sitting room, and almost collapsed into Gregor's armchair beside the desk where the little black telephone squatted, its disc glaring at her malignantly. While she was taking up the trumpet, the bell trilled again imperatively. She almost dropped the thing, but mastering her fears placed it to her ear, her unoccupied hand clutching at her throat meanwhile, as though to stifle her voice should she shriek with terror. She could feel her own fingers clutching there, bidding her be silent, as she listened to the harsh, guttural, unfamiliar voice so near, so near. She wanted to scream but she could feel her fingers clutching still tighter. The harsh voice spoke querulously, impatiently, but she could not understand what it was saying. She could only realise it was questioning her, harshly and imperiously in a foreign tongue. Still holding her throat tightly she replaced the trumpet with a trembling hand. The voice died away with a snarl. But the bell did not ring again.

For a long time Tamara sat motionless in the chair beside the desk, still clutching at her throat. When she did undress and go to bed it was only to lie frozen with terror through the long night waiting for the dawn, and Gregor.

It had happened three years ago. She had come from the south, alone, to Leningrad. Her parents were dead. She had had thoughts of going on the stage. And then, oh fool, she had lost her passport, all her papers. She had been arrested and charged with being a spy in German pay. She a spy! She did not know a word of German even. But what was the use? She could disprove nothing. The more vehement her protestations of innocence, the more did those men smile and wink at each other knowingly. 'Come on, sister,' one had said, 'you're pulling a good act, but it's no use.' 'Why not come clean and tell us? You'll probably only go to the mines for ten years,' another had chuckled. Ten years, my God! Ten years had already passed in those last couple of weeks. Ten years would be eternity. And the horrible, ghastly, incredible thing was that she felt that pretty soon she would confess! 'Yes, yes, I am a spy. Sure, I speak German. And what?' She could hear herself making the statement with a sort of cold intensity. Anything to get away from the mocking, relentless questioning, anything. And it was then that Gregor had appeared. Like an angel from heaven he had come. His profession as reporter took him almost everywhere. He had seen this poor, friendless, tortured girl and had had compassion upon her. Somehow, up to the present she didn't know how – she never wanted to know how – he had saved her. He stood surety for her, pitied her, loved her, married her. And since then she had been happy, though of one thing she was never sure. Gregor had never told her, but she felt it was so: he was never absolutely convinced of her innocence. Love overlooks many things. Gregor still believed she had been in German pay. But as much as he might believe that, he also believed she would never, never do such a thing again. For in standing as security for her Gregor had virtually pledged his life on her behalf. No, Gregor trusted her. There had been lovely, happy days; Sonya had come to them. She should have been altogether happy, but the memory of those racking days remained. Strangers terrified her. They might be secret agents. They might be trying her out. Her name was there, set down in their records for ever, suspect, a spy. Some day perhaps they'd try to get hold of her again. If only she was sure that Gregor knew, knew with absolute certainty she had never been a spy, could not speak a word of German even . . . then, then she felt with the utmost conviction, she would have the courage to fight, even when she was alone. And now tonight . . . the German voice over the phone! They were on her tracks again. Oh Gregor, Gregor! Through the long night. Would Gregor never come?

It was still dark, a grey November morning, when at last she heard his footstep on the stair. Gregor! Trembling, sobbing in his arms, she told him what had happened.

'And you could not distinguish what the voice said, Tamara?'

'No, it spoke in German. Oh, why, why should they try to catch me out like this, Gregor? Don't you see they were hoping I'd answer . . . trying to trick me?'

Gregor sat silent on the edge of the bed. He looked at Tamara intently. His eyes were kind, his voice grave. He spoke haltingly as though he could scarcely bring himself to speak the words.

'Answer me, Tamara. In me you have nothing to fear. You know that. Was the voice you heard . . . had you ever heard it before? Was it the voice of . . .' He stammered, his whole face twitched as though he were acting under some compulsion not of his own. '. . . I mean, was it the voice of one of the Germans you had . . . known . . . ?'

'Gregor!' Tamara's voice broke. 'You believe . . . ?'

Sonya, still asleep, stirred restlessly. Gregor leaned over and patted her tenderly. To Tamara his voice seemed a long way off when he spoke, a long way off, and in some queer manner it seemed as though what he was now saying had been said a long while ago, and he had gone on repeating it ever since: 'I do not know. I do not know.'

He paused. Crouching now at his knees she could feel her heart breaking. He did not know! Could he not feel?

Gregor spoke again. 'I try to believe . . . I try . . . Tell me, Tamara mine, you know that, don't you?'

She nodded wretchedly. Yes, he tried. It was some consolation. She pressed his knee with twitching fingers. But then, he didn't believe. She broke into a passion of weeping.

'There, there.' He tried to hold her up, to caress her, to soothe her. 'I believe you . . . I think I do . . .'

But she leapt from the floor and took up Sonya who, waked by her mother's crying, had now joined in with a puzzled sympathetic wail. Drying her tears Tamara set about her morning duties. Gregor slipped into some old clothes and took Sonya on his knee and patted her fair curly hair as he always did when she cried.

'I have not the courage to go through with this,' Tamara thought. 'Oh Gregor, believe in me! I need your belief, your trust, your strength.'

All day Tamara hoped and prayed, but even while she did so she felt it was all in vain. Gregor eating his breakfast, playing with Sonya, supine now on the bed trying to get a few hours' sleep . . . Gregor only *tried* to believe. And outside in the secret nerve-cells of the city they were plotting to catch her. She could see their faces. 'Think we'd forgotten you, sister? You'll come back and go for your trip to the mines.' Waiting, watching . . . 'We never forget, sister. We'll get you yet.'

When Gregor bade her goodnight on his departure to the office she held him tight to her. She could feel him trying, forcing himself almost, to believe her.

'Tamara mine, I'm sorry. Forgive me.'

But she had nothing to forgive. It was so.

'Should the phone ring . . .'

'Yes, Gregor?'

'Leave it. Don't go to it.' Then, kissing her and looking into her eyes steadily with the kind, grave glance she loved, 'We'll talk this over together, dear. Don't let it worry you. Be brave.'

And now he had gone. All night she waited for the telephone to ring. Or to hear a knock at the door. Perhaps the owner of the voice would appear in person. And behind him, in the dark hallway . . . 'Come on, sister, we've got you this time.' But no bell rang.

All night she lay awake waiting. Till again the grey November morning and Gregor. And so on for days. Possibly a week, but it might have been a lifetime. Gregor's nerves, too, were frayed. He loved her so much he had become infected with her terror. Gregor, too, waited for the inevitable. And this time there would be no one to save *him*.

This thought grew upon her day by day. For if she was arrested it would mean the end of Gregor's career. He'd have to go too. And Sonya? What would become of her?

She made up her mind. She'd kill herself. Tomorrow when Gregor returned he'd find the letter. The river was close by. Deep and cold. An unhappy solution, but still a solution. Tomorrow. She should write the letter tonight.

That day they went for a walk, the three of them. Dark and grey the huge buildings towered above the snowy streets. They walked past the shop windows. To her it was all terrible. Every face that looked at them might be the one. Every now and then she would glance over her shoulder. Surely they were being followed. At last they left the busy thoroughfare and turned down a side street. It was darker there but silent. No one passed them by. Here, at any rate, there was no one following them. Gregor with little Sonya in his arms turned to her.

'Tamara, I . . . I am afraid!'

'I know, darling, I know.'

'If they come for you again, I cannot save you. I, too, will have to pay the penalty.'

Tamara could not answer. She longed to tell him what she had decided, but that would have been of course impossible. Gregor continued.

'I have thought it all out. I will not let you be tortured again. I will not. And I do not wish to go on without you.'

'Oh Gregor, God bless you,' her heart said.

'They will not get us.' He paused and looked at Sonya who with arms spread wide was catching the falling snow flakes, catching them and watching them fade into nothingness in the rosy hollows of her little palms. 'I have decided.'

'Yes, Gregor?'

'I shall not go to the office tonight. I have made other arrangements. Tonight we – you, I and . . .' he could not trust himself to utter her name, only clasped Sonya more closely to him, 'tonight we say goodbye. Tonight we go out . . . into the darkness.'

'Gregor, Gregor!' There were blinding tears in her eyes. But her heart beat stronger with a feeling that was unaccountably like joy. She could hardly hear herself speak: 'You love me like *that*, Gregor?'

Gregor's eyes . . . so kind, so sad. He nodded. 'It is best. It is the only way. It solves all.'

There was no occasion for words any more. They walked on through the falling snow.

'If only he believed, I could die without regrets,' she thought. And then: 'Though he doesn't, yet he will still die with me.' Closer and closer to Gregor she pressed her body all the way home.

Gregor put Sonya carefully, tenderly in bed and bent over and kissed her. Tamara watched him, the tears scalding her eyes. But she must be brave. She turned away. In the sitting room a postcard lay on the floor. They hadn't noticed it when they entered. She stooped and picked it up. It had been posted in the city. It was addressed to Gregor in an unfamiliar handwriting. She looked at it closely. A few lines scribbled in a foreign language . . . She turned swiftly and ran with it to her husband.

Gregor turned slowly, looked at her terror-blanched face and then at the card.

Tamara watched him closely. Perhaps . . . the final ruse. Oh, they were cunning! They'd do anything . . . anything. Gregor seemed to take an unusually long time to read the few lines on the card. He seemed to be reading them over and over, uncomprehendingly, almost. Then, suddenly, inexplicably, he did the strangest thing. Tamara's mind could not comprehend all that followed. For he began to laugh, to laugh and sob at the same time, uncontrollably. He rushed at her, caught her in his arms and hugged her till she thought she must collapse. Then he began to dance, dragging her with him round and round the room. Sonya woke and instead of patting her head gently as he always did, he snatched her up and soon all three of them were mingled in one sprawling embrace.

At last Gregor set Sonya down and trembling in every limb began to speak.

'Tamara mine, all is well. We are saved. All is well, all is well.'

'But, how?' she questioned. 'I do not understand.'

Gregor pulled her down beside him.

'How could you, darling? I must explain. I have a friend. He is a Scotchman. I have not seen or heard from him for several years. He was one of those reporters who came over to Moscow with the Labour Mission. A nice fellow . . . you will like him, Tamara. And now he is back here, once again. Here in Leningrad. He is staying here a couple of weeks and wants to meet me again.

'A few evenings ago, he writes,' and here Gregor read: '"I telephoned you but could get no answer. Someone *did* take up the receiver, but though I called and called there was no reply."'

Gregor paused a moment. His eyes sparkled.

'My darling, don't you see? My friend speaks no Russian and of course must have spoken . . .' He broke off as though some new idea had just flashed into his mind.

'Then it was he who . . .' Tamara began.

But Gregor interrupted. He shouted. 'But of course, he spoke English, Tamara, don't you see? English!'

'I thought . . .'

'Yes, that it was German.' His eyes filled with tears. 'Tamara mine, will you ever forgive me for having doubted you?'

Tamara caught his head in her arms and held it close to her breast.

'Gregor, Gregor!'

'You know I always *tried* to believe . . .'

But Tamara held his head still closer so that the last words died away in a series of little muffled explosions.

'All is well: the terror has all gone now,' she whispered.

Shadows

I am writing you this, Richard, to implore your help. Although it is ages since I saw you last, you are the only friend I have; I have no link with the past but you. Nobody knows me here; they are all strangers; and though I suffer so, they will not heed me. They will not understand.

Our youth together – how far away is it? I do not know. And yet, fresher in my memory than the happenings of yesterday, lives the remembrance of the little wood and the cove where we used to sit and talk. You will remember that happy holiday we spent together just before we parted and that last conversation in the cove gazing over the restless sea. Did we part that day in anger? I forget. I forget so many things. And yet I must try to remember, try to piece together this life of mine, rather, these scattered fragments of life which mock me and seek to elude me. It is so tantalising: sometimes I fear my mind may break beneath the strain. Ah, no: I must put that thought from me. That must not, cannot be. The mind. What do you and I know of the mind, and of the vast forces which lie around us, in us and not yet wholly of us, secret, prowling, mysterious, fraught with such power as is beyond our knowledge, watching and waiting to encompass us, to overthrow what we call the seat of the reason – the mind whose powers and weaknesses we can never hope to comprehend?

You know that I was always reticent and retiring, a dreamer. After you had sailed away (was it very soon after? I am not sure), my father died and I was left alone in the old house by the woods. I suppose you heard he had left me well off, as they say. There was no need for me to work. I was thankful for that; I do not think my health would have been equal to withstand the rigours of the outdoor life which I had once planned with you, nor do I think my temperament would have been suited either to a commercial life or to the professions. I was glad to be independent enough to be alone. To lead my life as I listed, to be alone and to dream. A mistake perhaps; but there again you know what I was like: you know how for days and days, even in that far-off time when you knew me, I would avoid you, and, as you used to say, 'shut up' my mind to you. Ah, I remember now, it was one of those moody spells of mine that caused us to part in anger that day. You with your sane and hearty commonsense would not understand me; you despised me, thought me cowardly.

You called me a dreamer. So I was, and ever shall be. It was the old house, I think, that gave me the peculiar fancy that life itself was a dream. Yes, that house, so old, so very old, with the unforgotten lives of past generations of our family lying thick about it, in the large, sober dining hall, in the whispering corridors that ran their ghostly course around and about it, but, above all, in the room which was mine. That house, I say, and especially that room, moulded me, made me what I am. Born in the old house, from my earliest childhood I was aware of the strangeness of that particular room; its strangeness and its sinister beauty: they entranced me. In its gloomy recesses lay thick shadows which invaded me day by day, but at night, when all was silent and dark, the shadows thronged triumphant, whispering to me strange secrets, obscure and fleeting as my troubled dreams. Memories of some remote, ancestral past – what they were I knew not – but often in my childhood I have lain, feeling them crowding upon me, crowding remorselessly, whispering to me of my destiny, terrible and sure. My father knew of my fears and fancies, but with rough laughter bade me be a man. Cruel, cruel. Is he one of those dark shadows now? The very soul of my room, I sometimes think, must have entered mine as the years rolled on, and subdued me to its vast, impersonal force which awaited but the allotted moment to crush me utterly.

For many years I lived in the old house alone. I read and I dreamed. Looking back to that time, I cannot say that I was lonely; indeed I considered myself happy. And yet, in this mutability we call life, how may we designate happiness? It is only by our sufferings that we can appreciate happiness, and when that hour is vanished, its memory but makes our sufferings more intolerable.

So I lived in the old house alone. I do not think I had any visitors during my long seclusion. I wrote a little, but my subject was, I fear, too evanescent for me to grasp such an elusive theme. I cannot explain even now what it was I sought to discover: the mystery and beauty and dread of dreams, their subtle power acting and reacting upon our weak human wills, the link with the unsubstantial and indefinable – can I ever hope to explain? Perhaps a dream of dreams.

During those long years I had no companion but old Cato, my retriever. You will remember him. He loved me. During those brooding hours, when, seated at my desk in the old room, I strove to marshal my wandering thoughts, when I wrote far into the night, when the moon, pale and gibbous, shone through the bleak mullioned windows upon the wan sheets of my empty bed, and the shadows leapt and danced hither and thither as the swaying flame of the candle at my elbow made them, he sat at my feet and somehow strengthened me. Absurd, you will say, but I shared a strange communion with him. We understood each other.

I think it was his death that drove me to the outside world. I missed him; I became physically ill. I must have been ill for some time. Eventually the doctor forced me to seek a change. I demurred, but I was too weak to resist. I had been living too lonely a life, he said. I must mix with people, forget myself. The old house was closed. They took me to town.

After a while I began to feel stronger. I met people; I have forgotten them all; vague faces they remain in my memory. I actually dined out, danced. I think I was very ill then, more so than before I had left home. I was excited, tremendously excited, borne on by a nervous energy that was totally foreign to me. And more than ever I missed the old house and its mystery. I was flattered wherever I went. They knew I had money, more perhaps than any of them. They wanted me, the fawning mothers with their hot-house daughters; mine was the choice.

As you know, Richard, although no misogynist, I had never been attracted by women. Do you remember how you laughed at me that day when I ran away from your sister and her friends, ran away, and hid myself in the attic? But now, charged with that nervous excitability which possessed me, I felt a recurrent desire to acquire one of these products of the artificial society in which I moved. A desire to establish power over another human being, mine for the asking, urged me on. I was being driven on, I know now, to begin the working out of my destiny; the shadows bade me.

And so I made my choice. Let me try to recapture my impression of her when I met her first. It was her strangeness that appealed to me, a dark and wayward aloofness which seemed to scorn everyone, a passionate pride of spirit that lurked and peered, untamed and unafraid from those half-veiled eyes, a flame of unrest tormenting the fragile body that flitted like a firefly over the marches of the social circle that was ours. The swaying poise of her delicate body attracted me, her very disdain goaded me on. Baited with the social veneer that her mother had slabbered upon her, she played her part, and loathed and despised herself for it. I had the money. I bought her.

I had the old house redecorated. Thither we returned after our brief honeymoon.

◇

There was that occult sense within her too: an inexpressible sensitiveness that seemed to find in the old house something which she realised to be stronger than herself. Scornful, indomitable though she was, I knew that the spell had been cast upon her. What spell, do you ask me? I cannot tell you. She, too, had realised the unreal.

You could never understand the relationship of our married life. Urged on by some unknown power, I persisted in my wooing. She yielded me her kisses coldly, with deliberate disdain. That I did not mind, but I did mind that the secret of her soul should to me remain unread. The more I tried to fathom its dark meaning, the deeper did it recede from me, till it became lost in the labyrinth of her innermost self. Only the scorn, the ineffable scorn of her unfathomable eyes met mine. In the dark heart of the house I could feel her power; she encountered my soul, encountered and repelled it, overcame it and drove it reeling and conquered away. In my gloomy room, her room now, hers and mine, I would sit in the semi-darkness and watch her as she stared upon the changing heart of the fire, oblivious of my presence. Her mind was a sealed cipher; her body I had bought.

She seemed to prefer the seclusion of the house. Gradually our acquaintances drifted away from us and we were left alone. The death of her mother brought no tear of compassion or regret from her unflinching eyes. Before my marriage I had sometimes felt that I was on the track of the mystery which baffled me, but now I was like a rudderless ship in the ominous calm of the approaching typhoon of my fate. I was more than ever alone. And so was she. But the force of her will was such that never a word did she utter to betray the solitude of her soul. She suffered in the deeps.

I think I have said that she was frail. She grew frailer but the power in her grew. Grew, till I felt afraid of the smouldering hatred that shone in her eyes, a hatred which was now but dimly masked by her immutable scorn; and I knew that I too hated her. Why did I hate her? I hated the delicate perfumed body which I had purchased in the social mart, the unyielding mind that resisted and mocked me: above all, I hated her because of my ever having tried to win her. It was as though I hated in her all that I hated and despised in myself. But the hatred that festered in her – ah, in her it was stronger, deeper than in myself. In her it typified the revolt of the woman, the odalisque, the slave born and bred to be sold at auction to the whims and desires of the lustful ever-conquering male – it was the hatred of the sex which had degraded and enslaved her, a hatred fixed and rooted in her inmost self, a hatred old as the world, which had in its passionate intensity supplanted every other emotion that had ever existed in her embittered soul. And it was when she told me that she expected to bear me a child that I fully realised the implacable hatred blazing in her heart.

The months passed. Thank God, the child was born dead.

A few weeks had elapsed since her confinement, when one evening I was sitting by the window in the old room. The lights were low. She lay, a mere shadow, amid the deeper shadows of the bed.

And I resolved to kill her.

Yes, so much had I grown to hate and fear her. It would be very easy, thought I. There was no vitality in the wasted body; only the flame of her spirit brooded there. Fool I was to think I could slay that. Yes, a sudden sure grasp of that frail throat, and all would be over; I should be free.

I watched her narrowly. Her eyes were closed. Thinking she slept, I arose from my chair and approached the bed whereon she lay. Suddenly she opened her eyes and called my name. I drew back, and before she spoke I knew she had divined my intent.

'You fool,' she said, 'do you think to kill me? I, whom you, you and this accursed house have sought to destroy, will live for ever.'

She rose to a sitting posture. Her dark soul burned a channel through her eyes. Her cheeks were shadowed hollows; her neck a brittle stalk a child might snap. In the half-light I could read the scorn and sneer of her blanched lips.

'I have never known happiness, but you will – though not for long.'

She paused, fighting for breath, and I knew that my destiny depended upon the next words that I could see trembling upon the shrivelled lips.

'For I shall return to claim you.'

Her strength was ebbing; I knew that she was dying. But the forces of hell had been launched against me. I threw up my hands to ward off the curse as if it had been a tangible thing.

When I looked again, with her words still echoing in my ears, she had fallen back into a huddled mass and I knew that she was dead.

After her funeral I was more at my ease than I had ever been. Do you know, Richard, I actually took pleasure in mixing with others? The old house, somehow, seemed to have lost its hold upon me. I felt at the moment as though, by her death, its spell over me had been broken; perhaps, thought I, I had escaped its wrath through the sacrifice of the woman who had died. Never once did I experience aught of her presence. I remembered her valediction, true, but to my conscious mind it brought me no foreboding.

Time passed. I was stronger, healthier. I wanted to mix with my fellow men. I went to town and rented a small apartment. And then I met Elaine. Perhaps you too have loved; I know not. If you have not, it would be useless for me to try to explain the wonder and beauty of that time: if you have, you will understand. This was my happiness. I thank God for it: it was all I should know. How I loved her, my Elaine, with her sweet slow smile, her trustful eyes, mirrors of her fair soul, and the swift curve of her neck, dauntless and free! We met, we loved. There was no delay. We were borne on upon the crest of the wave that surged in our hearts, and in the exaltation of our mutual bliss, we saw no reason to wait. I cannot tell you how long a time elapsed between our meeting and our marriage. To me, in the shifting obscurity of the past, that time gleams swift and fleeting; a solitary star in a storm-tossed sky, one moment there, the next moment gone for ever: it might have been a month, a week, a day. Oh the memory of it, the memory.

We married. There was no elaborate ceremony. I have a recollection of us two, hand in hand, before the priest, the great church silent. And the happiness.

And there was no foreboding of the future. Strange I cannot account for that, I, who had been always so sensitive to such impressions. And why did I consent to take my bride to the old house? Now, alas, I realise my folly. I should have dissuaded her from ever going there, but she longed to know where I had lived. She knew the story of my youth and loneliness, of my unhappy marriage, and she desired to enter into that past cheerless life of mine, to dispel the gloom of the old place by the power of her love. I yielded to her plea when she asked me to return there after the ceremony.

It was already dark when we arrived. We had been so eager, it had been so sudden, this marriage of ours – I had had no time to have the house put in order; we should have to make the best of it awhile.

Black and almost animate it loomed in the starlight, menacing. Hand in hand we entered, and together we prepared and ate our supper. Here in the ancient dining hall its former gloom seemed to have disappeared, dispelled by the light of her innocence and love. I laughed at my former fears; the old house had been vanquished by a stronger power now that Love had ventured within its sinister doors. Yes, I was conscious that the shadows had been put to flight, and I told her how cheerful her presence had made the old hall. And she laughed and kissed me and looked into my eyes. Elaine, Elaine!

Why too did we decide to sleep in that room, that room of all others? I had shown her over the house, had heard her cheery laughter echo and re-echo throughout its grave and sombre fastnesses, and when she had chosen that room, I had not denied her choice. Had she even known its grim secret, she would still have dared. In her innocence she knew no fear, and from me too had she cast the shackles of the past.

I woke trembling, the clammy hand of fear upon my brow. I listened carefully. I could hear only the faint breathing of my bride, lost in slumber. The dying fire in the hearth cast grotesque shadows upon the wall. But – I could feel those shadowy presences, so well remembered, thronging about me, pressing upon me, hounded on by an implacable hatred which not even the grave might abate. Fool, to have thought I had escaped them! I could not move. I could hear once again those words of doom pronounced. I had returned to the pit predestined to engulf me. Of what avail hope, manhood, love? Down, down . . . This moment was, I knew, the prelude to the climax of my destiny. Now I glimpsed the meaning of the shadows, the dreams. My brain peered into the mystery of the unknown and recoiled reeling, sick, afraid.

And suddenly as I lay there, I experienced a perceptible change invade the heart of the room. Something mephitic and obscene, something too awful for the human mind to contemplate had taken place; what it was I dared not imagine. The sweat poured from me and a fit of nausea seized me. I could endure the terror of it no longer. I stretched out my hand to awaken Elaine. Her bare arm, thrown above her head, was deathly cold!

Shocked and choking with terror, I sprang from the bed, and fumbling in the semi-darkness, I lit the candle which stood by my bedside. By its feeble gleam I saw her huddled, drawn tense beneath the dim sheets. Her distorted appearance terrified me yet more. She looked . . . different.

I pulled her over roughly, turned her face to me.

Can I ever tell you, ever hope to convey to you the sense of the shock which palsies my hand even now as I write?

For the face which was turned to me, the wasted shoulder which I had grasped, were neither the face nor the shoulder of my bride, but of her, of her who had died, and dying had cursed me. And as my senses swam with the ghastly realisation of this unimaginable horror, I saw the half-veiled eyes open, saw the depths of the deathless hatred lurking there, saw the proud tormented scorn of the blanched lips, and heard the voice, mocking and bitter as the grave:

'Fool, your happiness is over: did you not think I would return?'

Blind with the nameless rage and loathing which seized me, I stretched out my hands and clutched the fragile throat which throbbed with unholy life.

'Where is she, my Elaine?' I shrieked.

But the mocking eyes, the mocking voice were mute.

Then slowly, slowly I choked the foul life out of her until I felt the body limp and lifeless in my grasp. Dead she was now, eternally.

And then . . . oh Christ! . . . how can I tell you? Slowly, by imperceptible degrees I saw the appearance of the corpse *change*. Those staring mocking eyes that had gazed into the gulf of hell assumed an expression mild and tender as the blue heavens above. The wasted form altered its proportions as I gazed down upon it, incredulous, and became clothed in perfect symmetry. The throat, the weak stalk that I had snapped, took upon itself the curve, the curve I had so loved, dauntless and free – the corpse had become the corpse of my beloved, my Elaine. And on the neck which erewhile I had so passionately kissed, there grew, deeper and deeper, the stark livid marks my fingers had made.

They took me away – when I know not, I who have lost all sense of time. Ages ago. They brought me here.

Richard, for God's sake help me, help me. They say that I am mad . . .

The Snag

Mark woke, stretched and yawned. At first he wondered where he was. He missed the iron rails and the solemn little brass knobs of his own bedstead. Then as he looked around the room, at the sloping roof of the attic with the myriad rusty twisted nails patterning its white-washed surface like so many unusual insects, at the battered chest-of-drawers, at the rickety tin washstand with its clumsy basin in which squatted a shameless naked ewer, he remembered he was spending a week with the Aunts.

And this was the second day. It was the first time his parents had allowed him to sleep away from home all by himself, and he was utterly and completely happy. Mother hadn't been keen on it, but Father had stood up for him manfully. 'He's getting to be a big boy now, dear.' (He certainly was, seven years old last Saturday!) 'You mustn't mollycoddle him too much. Besides, think how glad Jane and Judy will be to have him!'

Eventually it had all turned out satisfactorily. Not without a deal of incomprehensible fuss, Mother had brought him over yesterday and, after many last-minute instructions and embarrassing hugs and kisses, had gone, leaving him, for the first time, on his own.

Not that the place was strange, of course. Mark knew Graham Lodge almost as well as he knew his own home. He had often spent days there. The house, old and rambling, was a little distance out of town; there were odd corners and quaint unsuspected little flights of stairs almost everywhere; outside there was nearly an acre of orchard, garden beds and waste land – a thrilling country that bravely withstood the challenge of repeated exploration; there were so many things to be seen, so many things to be done!

Mark sat up. Now he could look right through the tiny window, over the roof, on to the tree-tops aback of the house. They were enjoying themselves immensely, tossing in the breeze like horses all harnessed up and waiting to be given the word go. Downstairs he could hear windows and doors being opened, voices and other sounds of matutinal activity. The call of the morning was too urgent to be disregarded. He scrambled out of bed and after a perfunctory toilet was soon stepping cautiously down the rickety stairs leading from the attic, lamenting on the way the fact that there were no bannisters to be slid down. He tiptoed past the bedrooms – Mother had warned him that Aunt Judy disliked her morning sleep disturbed – through the wide-open dining room, out on the wide brick verandah that faced east and south of the dining room. It was lovely out there. You could look over the bread-and-cheese hedge past the neighbouring trees to the low-lying hills beyond.

The wind was busy this morning. From the tall whitewood tree directly in front of the verandah it was wafting a flurry of little winged seeds that spun round and round in the air as though they were alive; it was causing the gate that led from the backyard to sway to and fro with a series of little cracks and explosions; and a rooster crossing the yard was undergoing a severe strain upon his dignity with all his tail-feathers blowing the wrong way. On Mark's right was the bit of waste land, situated in the hollow of an abrupt declivity. It had once been a marl-hole but was now chock full of thick bushes and weeds; a luxuriant growth of love-vine hung in crazy festoons from the taller bushes, and a few anaemic banana plants stuck up forlornly here and there among the wilderness. The Indians Mark had slain there! And the bears! He heaved a deep sigh of satisfaction. All this was his to enjoy for a whole week.

The backyard gate exploded with greater violence than usual, and a stocky well-built lad of thirteen or fourteen carrying two splashing buckets of water came through it.

Mark rushed down the verandah steps.

'Hello, Joe!'

Joe the yard-boy flashed a grin at him. 'Hey, Masta Mark, you up early enough.'

Joe was Mark's favourite at Graham Lodge. The Aunts were all very well in their way, and Cookie was nice and good-natured, and Martha the housemaid could be enticed to sing for you on occasions, but among all the inmates Joe was the only one you could be really chummy with. Of course Joe had numerous chores to perform and Aunt Jane saw to it that time never hung too heavily on his hands, but when Mark paid a visit it was understood that Mark had the right to claim him for some part of the day.

'Did they tell you I was going to be here for a whole week?'

Joe deposited the buckets and filled the watering-pot before replying. That was a provoking characteristic of Joe's. He was so deliberate in everything he did.

'Did they, Joe?'

'Miss Jane tell me yesterday. Thought you wasn't coming to look fo' we. An' Chris'mas come an' gone.'

There seemed to be some sort of implied reproof in this last remark which set Mark wondering vaguely, but just then Aunt Jane appeared clad in the heavy boots she always wore in the garden. 'Joe, Joe, what's become of you?'

Then she caught sight of Mark.

'Well, well, somebody's up very early! Have you had your tea?' And she proffered a lean cheek which Mark dutifully pecked.

'And did you sleep well, dear?'

'Uh-huh,' he replied, surreptitiously wiping his lips with the back of his hand. Such silliness, kissing.

'How many times have you been told not to say "Uh-huh"! Gracious, look at your hair!'

Unable to comply with her request he ran his hand through it; he was sure he had brushed it.

'You can't run around looking like that. Come here, dear.' And grasping his hand she led him up the steps, through the dining room into the large dark bedroom where the gigantic mahogany bedstead towered like a four-master at anchor. From the dressing-table bristling with mysterious bottles and pincushions she extracted a yellow pot-bellied brush and a sinister-looking comb.

'Please let me do it, Aunt Jane.'

Aunt Jane had a way of holding you under the chin and setting to work with such emphatic efficiency she'd often bring tears to your eyes.

'Nonsense, Mark. You never brush your hair properly.'

With a sigh Mark submitted. Aunt Jane was rather a problem anyway. She had little or none of the ineffective fussiness or submission to masculine whims so characteristic of grown-up ladies: there was something ruthless and forthright about her. Even her laugh, though she laughed but seldom, was gruff; Mark always pictured her in his private romances as the captain of a pirate ship. Yes, you had to watch your steps with Aunt Jane. It was she who issued all orders at Graham Lodge and, what was more, saw that they were obeyed. She was much older than his mother, as was also Aunt Judy. They were both unmarried, and Father referred to them as the two old girls. But whereas Father always pooh-poohed Aunt Judy's suggestions, he usually paid attention to what Aunt Jane said. When Mark visited Graham Lodge Aunt Jane was a perpetual reminder that one could not escape authority. Nothing was ever quite perfect; there was always a snag somewhere. Anyway, Aunt Jane's authority was a reasonable price to be paid for the joy of a visit to Graham Lodge.

'There,' she said at last giving a final whoosh of the brush to Mark's unruly curls. 'And so, you had a good night's rest?'

'Uh-huh.'

'I told you . . .'

'I mean, yes.'

'And have you been to say good-morning to Aunt Judy?'

'No. I thought she was asleep. Mother said . . .'

'No, dear, she's been up ever since. She's been reading her prayers.'

Aunt Jane ushered him into the adjoining bedroom. It was much smaller than Aunt Jane's, as was also the bed. Mark had often reflected how strange this was, for Aunt Judy was much larger than Aunt Jane; she was almost twice her size. She had a deal of fluffy faded brown hair, a round chubby face, and gracious, what an expanse of bosom! This was usually bedecked with an array of brooches from one of which, when she was neither reading nor crocheting, dangled a pair of pince-nez (or clips as Mark knew them), the bane of Aunt Judy's existence; for they often became entangled with the brooches, or else refused to stay for any appreciable length of time upon her nose.

She was sitting in a low armchair and reading from an unattractive moth-eaten volume entitled *Sermons from Stones*. She closed it as they entered, removed her clips, caught them on to one of the brooches and held out her arms.

'And how is my Diddums this morning?'

Her Diddums disdaining to reply let himself be embraced, keeping a wary eye on the brooches, then asked: 'Why stones, Aunt Judy?'

'Stones! . . . Oh, that's just a metaphor.'

'What's a met . . . meta . . .?'

This wasn't so easy to explain. 'Well, it's from Shakespeare. What he means is that one can find beautiful things in the most unusual places . . . music, for example . . . listen to the wind in the trees . . .'

'Come on, Judy, let's get tea,' interrupted Aunt Jane, ever practical, 'you'll be getting wind in your stomach presently.'

'Jane! Jane!' Aunt Judy's reproof was valiant, but she came out to tea with a protracted chuckle.

Early morning tea was perhaps a misnomer at Graham Lodge for they always drank coffee. Rich brown coffee and slices of crackly, thickly buttered toast that flew off in greasy crumbs when you bit into them and made a pleasant mess of your face and hands. They were so messy this morning that Aunt Jane's ministrations were again called upon and Mark found that the application of such a deal of soap spoiled the lingering flavour of the coffee: another of life's snags.

But out-of-doors he was soon carefree and happy. The gay beauty of the morning reacted upon his young spirits with appropriate effect. He raced, he romped, he danced, he sang, he shouted, he chased the rooster – pompous ass – he teased Cookie by making sorties upon her and slapping upon her broad wabbly hips when her back was turned; he enjoyed himself fully. He even persuaded Aunt Jane to surrender up Joe long before breakfast to play Indians in the marl-hole.

At breakfast he was ravenous. There was flying fish so thickly covered with breadcrumbs and egg batter that they seemed twice the usual size, coo-coo and okras, roast yam . . . He sighed with mixed feelings when it was all over. He'd had to refuse a second helping of guava jelly.

Aunt Judy wiped her lips with the large stiff napkin and leaned forward, her clips tinkling upon the empty tea cup.

'We're going to have a lodger, Mark. Did Mother tell you?'

A lodger! He looked up enquiringly. He didn't quite know what a lodger was.

'Yes, an old lady is coming to stay with us.'

'Who is she?'

'She's an old, old friend of ours. Papa and Mamma were very fond of her.'

Mark glanced at Aunt Jane. She was scowling, and at Aunt Judy's last remark she uttered a little grunt of annoyance.

'Have I said anything I shouldn't, Jane?'

'Stick to facts,' Aunt Jane replied.

'That's all over and past, Jane. Anyway she's coming to stay with us.'

'Why is she coming, Aunt Judy?'

'Because she's all alone. All these years she's been living with her sisters, but now they've gone.'

'Where, Aunt Judy?'

Aunt Judy pointed to the ceiling. Mark glanced up apprehensively.

'The Lord has called them home.'

Aunt Jane grunted again.

'She's very old,' Aunt Judy continued. 'She was very fond of . . . of Papa, and now she has nowhere to go. Nowhere.' Aunt Judy shook her head sadly.

'And when is she . . . due?' (Mark's father worked in a shipping office and Mark liked the expression.)

Aunt Judy smiled. 'She is not a vessel, dear, but she's due, as you say, this afternoon. Your Uncle William is bringing her over.'

'She's very old,' said Aunt Jane warningly.

'Very, very old,' emphasised Aunt Judy. 'You probably have never seen anyone quite as old as that before. You mustn't go asking her any questions. She's eighty-nine.'

Eighty-nine! Mark's eyes opened wide.

'She's rather hard of hearing,' Aunt Jane added, 'and she can't see very well.'

'Is she . . . is she alive?' asked Mark, and then blushed the moment he'd said it; it was so absurd.

Aunt Judy's titter was lost in the throaty guffaw that escaped from Aunt Jane.

'Alive! Of course she's alive.'

'The things a child says . . .'

'I meant . . .' But Mark couldn't quite express what he'd wanted to say. The conversation seemed to leave a vague sense of discomfort in some out-of-the-way corner of his mind.

He couldn't get Joe to play with after breakfast for the lodger's room had to be made ready. Aunt Judy was moving into the big bedroom with Aunt Jane and all sorts of things had to be shifted. This proved to be grand fun. It was thrilling to carry in old boxes and to catch fleeting glimpses of that hitherto unrevealed mystery, the contents of Aunt Judy's wardrobe; all the oddments and knick-knacks that the passing of the years had stored within those shelves in such prodigal variety. For in addition to mere prosaic garments there were stacks of letters, boxes, bags, bottles, scrap-albums, faded photographs of quaintly attired dead and gone relatives, scentless sachets, a mousetrap, a couple of curios from Mexico, an entrancing book with cuts of skeletons and people's insides which was quickly wrested from his grasp, broken china ornaments, an old rag doll . . .

Mark enjoyed himself immensely. Despite the fact that Aunt Judy was almost prostrated by excess of fussiness, and he was on several occasions ordered to leave the room, he wouldn't have missed it all for anything.

So the time passed swiftly and Mark was quite hungry again by luncheon time; he didn't refuse any jelly now, for he scraped the last shreds from the bottle.

After luncheon, all preparations made, they sat in the drawing room. Aunt Judy got to work on her crochet, stopping every now and then to readjust her clips which persisted in sliding stealthily off her pudgy nose, at times becoming entangled with the thread. Aunt Jane read and hummed a little tune in between. Mark lay on the carpet. There was nothing else to do, not for an hour or so at any rate. Joe had gone off on an errand and would not be back till four. Then Mark would dress and Joe and he would go out on the little strip of pasture aback of the house and . . . he looked over to Aunt Jane almost expecting her to divine his thoughts . . . pick dunks. Anyway, even if she forbade him to do this there were lots of other things to be done.

Mark found the drawing room faintly hostile, hostile and mysterious. It was not bright and cheerful like the dining room; there were no windows giving on the open sky. But it was cool, for the wind found its way in somehow and the heavy cretonne curtains swelled and bulged importantly. Everything in the room looked important and grown-up and alien. The curtains, the heavy chairs, the large faded pictures in their rusty gilt frames, the overweening glass epergne on the centre table, the ornaments – they all had a pompous, secretive air. The rug alone on which he now lay was open-hearted and friendly. He looked over at the massive chiffonier at the far end of the room. The elaborately carved chiffonier was the most important and unfriendly of all. It assumed undisputed sovereignty over all the other articles of furniture. When the big brass lamp overhead was lit and shadows lurked in the corners you couldn't play at Indians or Bears or anything like that, for you never knew what might hear your howls and come creeping, creeping softly from the dark recesses of the chiffonier to investigate . . .

'Four o'clock, Mark. Time to dress!'

Mark rubbed his eyes and jumped to his feet at Aunt Jane's words. Soon he was outside waiting impatiently for Joe to finish watering and then, away they scampered through the hedge and out on to the open pasture aback of Graham Lodge where they rambled, picking and eating their dunks to their hearts' content (Aunt Jane had forgotten to exact any promise from him). Then they lay in the sweet-smelling stubbly grass and Joe told stories of Brer Fox and Brer Rabbit.

The shadows lengthened, the sky changed from powder-blue to gun-metal, marauding bats were weaving a crazy pattern overhead . . .

When they returned Mark was greeted by Aunt Jane who was standing on the front porch.

'Wherever have you been, child? Uncle William wanted to see you before he left. Come on in and meet Miss Martha.'

'Who?'

'Don't you remember? The old lady. We girls always call her Miss Martha. Come along. Remember, she is very old.'

It was past six o'clock, and in the early January dusk the drawing-room lamp was shining wanly. In the far corner of the room beside the chiffonier a figure was seated, a figure that seemed too fantastic to be real. He came to an involuntary halt and had to be pushed on by Aunt Jane.

When they reached the figure Aunt Jane leaned forward and shouted into its ear: 'This is Mark, Miss Martha! Mark! Carrie's boy!'

Miss Martha's head moved slowly around. In the brief while that ensued between Aunt Jane's words and the movement of Miss Martha's head, a picture of her intense decrepitude was painted upon the screen of his memory, a picture that was destined to remain there for many a long year. He saw a huddled, almost shapeless creature clad in some shiny black material, the skirts of which stuck out all around stiffly in voluminous folds. From the lace collar of the dress protruded a small shrunken head upon whose sparse silver hairs was perched a little lace cap with black ribbons. The face was scored with countless criss-crossing wrinkles and was of the colour of wax. The blue eyes, sunk far back in their sockets beneath the bony overhanging brow, were covered with a strange whitish film; the withered, puckered mouth was trembling.

Miss Martha's head moved slowly around with a swaying halting movement. Mark clutched Aunt Jane's hand. He felt cold with terror.

'It's Mark, Carrie's son!'

A look of understanding passed over the blank, blind face. The lips mumbled.

'Carrie's son?'

'Yes, Miss Martha.'

With all his soul he prayed she wasn't going to kiss him. Oh God, don't let her, don't let her!

Possibly the prayer was heard, for Miss Martha stretched out a hand, hitherto concealed by a black shawl Mark had not observed, a wasted, gnarled hand upon which were bunched snaky bluish veins that seemed to have been pasted on upon the withered flesh.

The hand moved blindly towards him. 'How are you, little Mark?'

Despite his horror Mark detected a kindly note in the croaking voice.

Aunt Jane gathered the groping hand into one of hers and with the other pressed Mark's into it.

But for the kindly tone of Miss Martha's voice he would have cried out aloud at the impact of that clammy grasp.

'How are you, little Mark?'

He saw the quavering lips take upon them the tracery of a smile.

'Well, thank you, Miss Martha,' he heard himself saying.

Miss Martha's other hand came out of its hiding-place and passed tremblingly over his hair.

'A nice curly-headed boy, Carrie's boy,' she mumbled, turning her sightless eyes towards Aunt Jane.

Mark felt his insides being torn between horror and a strange nameless sadness. Tears came into his eyes.

Aunt Jane touched him on the shoulder.

'There, run away, dear. Go and call Aunt Judy for me.'

He was unusually silent for the remainder of the evening. Miss Martha was led to her room early and did not dine with them. Aunt Judy explained she had to dine early; besides, she had to have her meals taken to her.

After dinner Mark did not go into the drawing room; it was more hostile than ever tonight. When the table had been cleared and the reading lamp set upon its chequered red and brown cloth he remained there looking through some old illustrated papers till bedtime.

Aunt Jane went upstairs with him, helped him put away his clothes, reminded him to say his prayers, tucked him in bed and bade him goodnight.

He fell asleep almost immediately . . .

He woke in the middle of the night. The moon had risen and the room was filled with an unusual pale radiance. He had been dreaming. Miss Martha had been chasing him round and round the house. At last she had caught him and had sat upon his stomach. He could feel her there still. He was terrified. He wished he was back at home. He began to cry. He tried not to. But soon he had forgotten he was a big boy and was yelling at the top of his voice: 'Mother, Mother, don't let her!'

Presently Aunt Jane opened the door, set down the oil lamp upon the chest-of-drawers and, unusually large in her long night-gown, was bending over him.

'Mark, Mark, whatever is the matter?'

The strangeness of Aunt Jane's attire and the novelty of seeing her hair done up in two spiky plaits reassured him somewhat. The crying stopped, but big sobs came up and burst inside him.

'Miss Martha,' he managed to say. 'She was chasing me.'

'Nonsense, Mark, you've been dreaming.'

He continued to sob and Aunt Jane smoothed his hair. She sat with him for a long time till at last he no longer felt frightened. Strangely enough he wasn't sleepy. He wanted to talk.

'Aunt Jane, does everybody have to get old?'

'Well, we all like to live as long as possible.'

'But do we have to get old like Miss Martha? Do we?'

'Not always. But never mind that now.'

'But do we, Aunt Jane? Will you get old like that? And Mother? And Father? And me?'

Aunt Jane fidgeted. 'Go to sleep, dear. It's very late.'

'But why do we have to get old and look like that? It's awful, Aunt Jane.'

'Go to sleep, there's a good boy. Very few people ever reach that age.'

Mark was silent for a little while.

Then: 'I hope I shall die pretty young, Aunt Jane.'

'Nonsense, nonsense. Go to sleep.'

Again Mark was silent. But his stomach began making gurgling noises, so he rubbed it contemplatively.

'Have you got a pain in your tummy?'

'Miss Martha sat on it.'

'Mark!'

'Yes, Aunt Jane?'

'You've been eating dunks again!'

'Yes, Aunt Jane.' Very faintly.

'Many?'

He considered the question drowsily. It couldn't have been Miss Martha after all. It must have been the dunks. How old Miss Martha was, though! She was old, old, very old . . .

'How many did you eat, child?' Aunt Jane insisted. Really, how anyone could eat those horrid frothy things . . .

Yes, Miss Martha was old, old, old . . . very old . . . she was . . .

'Eighty-nine,' he murmured as he dropped off to sleep.

'My God!' ejaculated Aunt Jane. 'Really, Mark, I must forbid . . .' she began. But on hearing his deep regular breathing she broke off and a smile spread over her stern old face. She stooped over and kissed his forehead.

She straightened herself, crossed over to the window and looked out upon the silent beauty of the night. She sighed. Mark's questioning had come as a grim reminder of the toll taken by the passing years. Not so long ago she had seen Miss Martha on just such a night as this dancing with Papa. She had been beautiful even then. Well, it was for Papa's sake she was with them now. And in a few years' time, she too, if she didn't die in the meantime, she too would be an old, old woman like Miss Martha. Time spared nobody.

She came back to Mark's bed and looked down at him. He was so young, so full of life. And downstairs, Miss Martha! And poised between the two but slipping dangerously fast over to the wrong side, herself. Life was very beautiful, but there was growing old, decay, death. No wonder poor little Mark had been so terrified. Ah, well, there was always a snag somewhere. She took up the lamp, gave Mark another glance, closed the door behind her and went downstairs.

Miss Edison

How on earth could I have made the mistake? I was pretty certain that my brother-in-law had said he'd be able to see me at eight o'clock. Now the maid informed me he was expecting me at nine. Well, well, and I had so many things to do. I was going back home tomorrow. An hour to wait . . . I lit my pipe and looked around. Bill's living room was cluttered up with books and magazines, but I didn't feel like reading. It was a beautiful sunny morning and out-of-doors was more enticing, even though it happened to be all enclosed by high walls, and the walls of a mental hospital at that. Perhaps I should have mentioned before that Bill was the resident psychiatrist and that I'd come to bid him goodbye before returning to British Guiana.

I descended the steps of the bougainvillaea-shaded verandah and strolled down the gravelled pathway leading from Bill's quarters. The sky was flecked with hurrying wisps of cloud and the tall cabbage-palms were swaying overhead and rustling fussily. It was all very beautiful indeed. As I reached the end of the pathway one of the male assistants passed and touched his cap. Bidding him good-morning I was thinking of all the blighted lives enclosed by these high forbidding walls. Blighted, lost lives . . . I didn't see any of the inmates anywhere, only . . .

A young lady approached. A nurse was walking beside her and the two were chatting together in a friendly way. The young lady suddenly became aware of my presence, bowed and smiled.

The moment she smiled I recognised her.

She came forward and extended her hand. 'Why, how do you do?'

'Fancy meeting you here, Miss Edison!'

I had met Sylvia Edison some four or five years ago in BG and had rather liked her. It was pleasant to think she still remembered me.

It was only after I made my somewhat fatuous remark that I realised with a shock that in all probability she was . . .

I glanced at the nurse whose answering look confirmed my suspicions.

But Miss Edison wasn't at all embarrassed. 'Yes, fancy meeting me here. Won't you sit down?'

She indicated a green garden-seat in the shade of the hibiscus border.

I glanced at the nurse again. She nodded.

'It's all very terrible,' Miss Edison said as she sat, 'but I'm sure you'll understand when I tell you the whole story.'

She arranged her frock with a hurried, nervous gesture and smiled at me. She looked rather pretty sitting there, I thought. She wasn't beautiful by any means: her features though well-formed were inclined to be . . . well, a little severe; but she possessed a very attractive figure. Her hands were small and delicately made. I noticed they were seldom still, and I remembered a little way she had of rubbing her thumb-nails together in a nervous schoolgirlish manner when she was excited about anything. She was rubbing them together now.

'I think I should tell you the circumstances,' she began.

'Oh, but it's not really necessary,' I assured her. 'I'm quite . . .'

But she had no intention of letting me interrupt her.

'No, I must tell you. You ought to know. Everyone ought to know.' She glanced around apprehensively. 'There have been such rumours, such lying rumours.'

The nurse withdrew a few paces and sat on the low stone border that ran along the path.

'You know that my sisters are here too?'

I'd not been aware she had any sisters. I said so.

'Weren't they with me in BG?'

'I . . . I don't think so.'

She drew her hand across her brow and closed her eyes for a moment.

'Really, you must forgive me. Such a lot has happened. I forget things at times. And I was almost certain they were with me on my holiday.'

'If they had been I should most certainly . . .'

'Well, perhaps you're right.' She sighed, a little sigh of relief it seemed like, and looked up at me, a bit archly, I thought.

'So you never met them?'

'No. I've only been here . . .'

'Poor Blanche! Poor Thora!' She shuddered as she mentioned the latter name. 'Well, let me try to get things all straightened out for you. There were three of us, Blanche, Thora' (again the shudder) 'and myself.

'Dad died when we were very young, you know, and Mum was all we had. Mum was very sweet to us. Then three years ago . . . that was after I returned from BG . . . she died.'

I knew nothing whatever of Miss Edison's family history. I had met her three or four times, danced with her, played a couple of sets of tennis with her as my partner, and there my acquaintance ended. A friend of mine had told me she was rather hot stuff, but I'd always found her . . . well . . . prim, if anything. There was a sort of schoolmarmish atmosphere about her.

'Yes, Mum was very sweet to us. She . . . she kept the peace between us, for we never got along very well together.' She was rubbing her thumb-nails against each other more busily now. 'You see, we were not very loving sisters. I must confess, I don't think anyone would have imagined we were all children of the same parents. Sometimes I've even thought . . . but no, that's wrong of me, wrong.'

I remembered her when she said the word 'wrong' as she'd looked that evening at the dance when I'd put my arm around her while we were sitting out. Prim, that was the word.

'You see, Blanche was always so weak-willed. You'll pardon my mentioning the fact, but we're grown-ups after all; I mean, she always thought such a lot about sex, even when she was a little girl. She . . . she disgusted me. You've no idea the awful things she used to tell me. But she wasn't a bad girl, please understand. She was loving and sympathetic. It was that I just didn't like that sort of thing. But I liked Blanche.' She paused and smiled reminiscently. 'But Thora . . .' She closed her eyes and shuddered again. 'She always hated me. She hated Blanche too. Both of us. She seldom spoke a word to us. She had a frightful temper too, frightening. Only Mum could control her, and when Mum died . . . Oh, it was awful being left alone with her.'

She broke off, overcome by the recollection, and I tried to tell her not to worry to go on with her story if it caused her so much pain, but she ignored my faltering attempt and continued.

'And so we grew up and . . .' she glanced up at me, giggled, a peculiar unexpected giggle, 'and entered womanhood. I think the strain of living with my sisters had undermined my health. That's why Mum said we should go away for a change. That's how we happened to go to BG.'

'But your sisters didn't . . .'

'Of course, how silly of me, I remember now. I refused to go if the others went, so I went alone.'

She paused and sighed.

'I had a wonderful time. It was the loveliest time of my life. Alone, without Thora, without Blan . . .' She broke off and looked at me searchingly.

'So you never met Blanche?'

'My dear Miss Edison . . .'

'Ah, of course you told me.' She leaned forward, lowered her voice and asked with intense earnestness: 'Wasn't I a nice girl? I mean, didn't you like me?'

'Why . . . yes . . .' I stammered, 'I thought you were a very . . .'

But the moment she had asked the question she ceased to attach any importance to whatever I might have answered. 'Oh, if only I'd been able to remain there.' She clasped her hands close. 'All this would never have happened.' She unclasped them and again the thumbs got to work. 'No sooner had I returned when Mum died. It was awful . . . awful! Now I had nobody. Alone with Blanche . . . alone with Thora . . .

'Blanche was no good. She was . . . oh, the fellows she used to go around with! All hours of the night. Mum wasn't there and she wouldn't listen to me. I used to implore her, I did all that was humanly possible, I assure you, to make her realise the shamefulness of the life she was leading. But it was no use. Sometimes she'd say, "Sylvia, I'm so ashamed of myself." Poor Blanche! And the long nights she'd leave me alone with . . . her . . . Thora, I mean. I don't know how I didn't go out of my mind. She hated me so. My only consolation was I knew she hated Blanche even more. How could anyone hate Blanche? She might have been wanton, but she had a dear, tender heart. How long this might have gone on, I don't know, but then the unexpected happened.'

She paused and looked away.

'Can you guess?'

I said I hadn't an idea.

'Blanche fell in love. And the boy was in love with Blanche too. I knew. I could see. Even poor little me who'd had no experience in matters of this sort, I could see.' She giggled again in that peculiar unexpected way.

I don't know why, but there was something particularly revolting in that giggle of hers; it wasn't in keeping with that primness I'd learnt to associate with her. I stirred uneasily.

'Yes, they were in love. Oh, it was wonderful, wonderful!'

For the first time since she had begun her story her hands were still. Her face was radiant. For the space of a few seconds she remained like this, her prim, restless little face transfigured as she gazed out over the feathery palm trees into the past.

Suddenly the fingers began to move again. 'But Thora . . .' Her voice trembled with passion and a sudden wave of hatred swept over her face; I could hardly imagine that only a few seconds ago its expression had been so rapt.

The nurse coughed. Miss Edison glanced at her, caught her eye and taking a deep breath continued: 'The heartlessness of her! Do you know what she said when she heard that Blanche and Ian . . . that was his name . . . were going to be married? She said she'd tell Ian all about Blanche . . . everything. About Harold and Jim and Gerald and that time she'd had to . . . Oh it was horrible. We pleaded with her. "It's never too late," I said. "Now that Blanche is in love she'll turn over a new leaf, I'm sure." But she was adamant. She only sneered at my pleading. "I've sworn," she said, "I've sworn that no decent man shall ever make a mess of his life for that . . ." and she used a vile word. "He'd better be dead." That was what she said. "He'd better be dead."

'And then . . . I remember the night. Ian had come to take

Blanche to the pictures. "Well, I've got the licence," he said. Instinctively I looked across at Thora. She was sitting by the radio. She got up and walked over to where Ian was standing. "So you've got the licence," she repeated. "You bet," Ian answered, and he began fumbling in his pocket for it. I saw Thora turn and walk out of the room. I felt that something awful was going to happen. I didn't say anything. I just sat still, waiting . . . The others didn't seem to notice anything. Ian had gone over to the window and was looking out into the night. Blanche had come over to me and was saying something. I didn't pay any attention to her. I seemed to be in a dream . . .

'And then Thora came back. She was holding something close to her. I couldn't see what it was. She crossed over to Ian. His back was to her. She was standing right behind him now. He was unaware of her presence. I could see the smoke from his cigarette floating out through the window . . . out into the darkness. Blanche was still talking to me, talking . . . And I couldn't say a word, I couldn't move. And then . . . Thora raised her hand and brought it down. There was a knife in it . . .'

The nurse rose, came over to Miss Edison and patted her gently on the shoulder.

'There now, dearie, that'll do.'

Now that the climax of the story had been reached, its narrator was strangely still. The busily moving hands lay folded like two birds that had come home from flight. She was gazing into vacancy.

Soon her lips moved again, but the hands remained motionless.

'If the shock had a great effect upon me, you can imagine how it affected Blanche! It deranged her mind, poor thing. So they sent her here. I had to come with her . . . naturally.'

She paused, motioned to the nurse to move away as if for the first time she had become conscious of her proximity, and looked around her in a scared sort of way. Her voice sank to a whisper.

'They sent *her* here too. She should have been hanged. Murderess!' She hissed out the word, and again her face was distorted by an expression of indescribable hatred.

The nurse, who hadn't moved away, patted her on the shoulder, this time not quite so gently.

Miss Edison made a gesture of annoyance, but she resumed her normal tone. 'But her lawyer pleaded insanity. Oh, he was clever, her lawyer. And such a nice young man!'

Again that revolting giggle. I edged away involuntarily.

'Yes, he saved her life. And so we're all here, all three of us . . . Thora . . . Blanche . . . Sylvia . . .'

And then she began to laugh. God, it was horrible! Peal upon peal of obscene, inhuman laughter.

The nurse helped her to her feet and led her away still laughing.

What a tragedy! Talk of blighted lives . . . I felt physically exhausted. Though it was so early I'd have to ask Bill to give me a drink. Hello, here he was!

'I see you've been talking to our Miss Edison. Gives you the willies, doesn't she? Well, who was she today, Blanche, or Sylvia, or Thora?'

'You mean . . .?'

'Oh, she killed poor Ian Carpenter all right, did Blanche Sylvia Thora Edison. You've heard of Jekyll and Hyde no doubt. Well, our Miss Edison goes one better. The human mind is a queer contraption. Better come and have a gin-sling.'

Miss Edison and her nurse had disappeared by now, but I could still hear in the distance, peal upon peal, her maniac laughter.

Twin-Ending

I looked at my watch. It was a minute to ten, and despite the earliness of the hour and the presence of my charming hostess, I felt confoundedly sleepy. A long whisky and soda too soon after dinner usually has that effect. Moreover I was piqued.

Jean noticed my action. 'You're surely not thinking of going yet! Why, whatever will Joan say? The picture'll soon be over now.'

I leaned back and extinguished a yawn.

'I really don't know why I should be so hopelessly . . .'

'In love? I know, I know. But even if you haven't seen her for so long, don't tell me you're going to make a bolt of it at the last moment. Do you find me so very boring?'

'Rot, Jee. It's just that . . . that . . .'

'I'm sure she couldn't have got your message, darling. Why worry? She'll soon be here now.'

Perhaps a word or two of explanation is necessary here. Jean and Joan (Jee and Jo to their friends) were twins, and I'd known them for a long time. Joan had been away for the past eighteen months improving her acquaintance with art; Jean meanwhile improved the occasion, so difficult when they were together, by marrying Phil. I'd also known Phil for years: one of the best. And Joan had just returned and was staying with them. I . . . I was fond of the twins, especially Jo. As to being in love . . . well, you know what women are like, always matchmaking, and Jean was convinced I'd come there that night bursting with a proposal of marriage, to say the least. And Joan had gone to the theatre . . . her first night home . . . with Phil. I was damped.

'Sulking like a ten-year-old.'

'I'm not, but . . .'

Jean laughed. 'You never were a good liar.'

'A successful liar, you mean.'

I settled back more comfortably. Confessions are so soothing to the soul. I felt quite wide-awake now. Perhaps she hadn't got my message after all.

'What picture have they gone to?'

'*Crooked Answers*. At the Empire. I've seen it already but Jo hasn't. And she was so keen on seeing Malory Dean. It's the last night and he's her special favourite. Not a bad film, but Malory Dean's love-making gets on my nerves. I couldn't make it a second time, not even for Jo.' She grimaced.

'I agree. These intense love themes are embarrassing.'

'Funnily enough, Jo never got a chance to see it in the States; now, thanks to the time lag, she has.'

'I can't say I thought much of *Crooked Answers*. That scene . . .'

But Jean interrupted what I had intended to be quite a scathing criticism.

'It's funny how Jo and I never seem to agree on pictures, you know. I mean we have pretty similar tastes in almost everything else.'

I was about to make a flippant comment.

'Well, I like *you*, you boob, at any rate. But Malory Dean . . .' She grimaced again. 'I hate that dreadful purring way of his. And those loathsome semi-circular moustaches . . .'

'Yes, it's queer you disagree. But it's even queerer that you agree upon all the others. It's a queer thing anyhow, this twin business. Just an unaccountable freak in the cell-division of the embryo, and one individual, June shall we call her, becomes Jean and Joan.'

Jean placed a cigarette between her lips and leaned forward for me to perform one of those quite unnecessary masculine duties.

'Ummm,' she agreed, 'it's very queer. You know, I've never been quite able to understand it. I don't mean the physical resemblance, or even the little mannerisms we share. No, it's lots of other things . . . mental, psychical . . .'

She threw her head back, and the smoke spiralled around and above her. She looks charming when she's smoking. So does Jo.

'Such as?'

'Well, of course, we don't notice it so much now. But before . . .

when we were small . . . I mean, we used to think practically the same thing. For example, what do you say to this? We'd come downstairs on mornings and sit at the little round table for tea. Then Mother might say, "Well, dearies, any dreams last night?" And we'd begin. Jo would start the ball rolling and then I'd chime in . . .'

'You're not telling me you both dreamt the same thing!'

Jean nodded. 'That's what I'm telling you. Jo would say something, then I'd pick up and put in some detail she'd omitted or forgotten, and so on till we'd given Mother the whole works.'

'Honest, Jee?' I asked. 'I mean, you didn't sort of improvise as you went along?'

Jean laughed. 'I'm not even a *poor* liar, dear. No, we just dreamt the same thing, that's all. Why, I remember once . . .' She broke off, took a last pull at the tiny rose-red stub, rubbed it meditatively in the ash-tray and shook her head. 'That one was rather terrifying . . . and we decided never to tell anyone about it. But we've not had a twin dream now, except that one, for years and years.'

Years and years! The twins were only just out of their teens.

'As I was saying,' she continued, 'the dreams stopped off, but for a long time afterwards we still seemed to think the same things. Perhaps I'd be thinking of . . . oh, going for a sea-bathe, say, and I'd hear Jo call, "Do you think Mother will let us stay on after the bathe for matinee?" or something like that.'

'But . . . but didn't you find that pretty awful? Fancy someone listening in like that on you! Fancy somebody knowing what I was thinking about sometimes! My God, how awful!' I wriggled uneasily.

Jean giggled. 'We were rather nice little girls. We never thought about it. We just took it as a matter of course. It was only after we grew up that we realised how unusual it must have been.'

'But don't you still?'

'No. That is, very seldom. Hardly ever, in fact.'

A car drew up outside.

'That's them now,' said Jean. 'Well, let's go and meet them.'

We rose and went out on the verandah. But it wasn't them after all. The car, whosever it was, started up again and went on. Jean sat upon the balustrade and lit up another cigarette. She smoked in silence.

I watched the cars passing for a little while.

Presently she spoke. 'You really do love her, don't you?'

I made a vague sort of noise.

But Jean didn't appear to be concerned with my reaction to the question, as her next remark showed.

'Oh, you don't know how much I love Phil!'

'After all, you've only been married . . .' I began.

'Silly. It's not a question of time. It gets worse and worse, as a matter of fact.'

'Or better and better?'

'Or better and better. But sometimes it's rather frightening. Tonight, for instance, I can't tell you how I'm longing for him . . . It's . . . it's positively indecent. Why, I feel as if . . .'

'As if . . .' I prompted. I might get some idea how Joan would feel under similar conditions. But I didn't want to appear too eager, so I put the question in a casual sort of way. I wouldn't look at her; instead, I leaned forward and began fumbling with one of my shoe laces, expecting intimate revelations.

Then a most surprising thing happened. A thing I'd never seen before. Something fell on the floor of the verandah with a soft plop and a shower of sparks. It was Jean's cigarette, barely a third of it smoked, and I'd never known Jean to let that much of a cigarette go begging, much less drop one. I looked up at her.

She was sitting rigid, and she seemed to be seeing something that wasn't there. Just sitting there as if she was made of stone, and staring past me into nothingness. There wasn't a sound. The cars had all gone past by now. I was frightened.

'Jee,' I said, 'Jee, what's the matter?'

Her lips moved. She seemed to be trying to say something.

'Jee,' I said again, 'are you ill?'

And then she spoke. I'd never heard Jean speak like that before. It wasn't so much the words, but the tone in which she said them.

'The bitch, the little bitch,' was what she said.

And then she collapsed. Passed right out.

I grabbed her before she fell and somehow managed to get her over to the settee. I rubbed her hands, thought of telephoning her doctor, but couldn't remember if it was James or O'Dowd, tried to fan her with a cushion . . . Finally I poured out a good shot of rum, and after a little trouble, got most of it down her throat.

After a while she came to.

'Have . . . have they come yet?'

'Not yet, dear.'

She seemed relieved to know this, and she smiled. A wan sort of smile.

'Sorry, old boy,' she said as she sat up slowly. 'Sit down and give me a cigarette.'

I did so.

She leaned back and inhaled luxuriously. Then she looked at me and I saw her eyes filled with tears.

'OK, dear?' I enquired anxiously.

'OK,' she replied. But her hands were trembling.

'Jee, dear, I don't want to appear inquisitive, but whatever's the matter? Can I do anything?'

She didn't answer immediately. Only her lips tightened and she frowned. She puffed on a while in silence. Then she turned to me.

'I suppose I'd better tell you. Yes, I think so. Remember our conversation just before we went out on the verandah?'

I nodded.

'Well, afterwards when we were sitting out there I began to tell you how I loved Phil. I said I couldn't try to tell you how much I loved him, how I was longing for him . . . remember . . . positively indecent . . . yes, that was it . . .'

I nodded again.

'Well, just as I was trying to explain it to you . . . my God . . .' She stopped and drew a long shuddering breath. 'Just then I realised it . . . I realised it all. I knew.'

'Knew what?'

'That it wasn't *me* thinking this. It was *her*. It was Jo!'

'Jo!'

'Don't you understand? The theatre's been over ages now. It was Jo. Jo thinking all that about Phil. Jo! I was listening in . . . Jo, darling, how could you?'

Joan . . .

Then she broke down completely and sobbed. Sobbed and sobbed.

I tried to comfort her. Not with much success, I fear.

At last she sat up and dried her eyes.

'I'm sorry I called Jo that awful name. I didn't really mean it, you know.' She shook her head sadly. 'Oh, but the horrid part is, I did. Jo's Jo, after all.'

Yes, Jo was Jo.

'And she always loved Phil . . . Sorry, dear . . . I suppose it's just as much my fault as hers. Marrying him like that when she was away . . .'

I didn't know what to say.

It was after midnight when the car drove in.

And now for the conclusion. You can take either you please. If you're in favour of the happy ending, you'll probably like (A); if, on the other hand, you don't, you'll perhaps prefer (B). I don't know, as it's quite possible you'll like neither. But then, I rather like the title of the story.

So . . .

(A)

We heard Phil's voice long before he entered. 'Hey, where are you, Jee?'

By the time he appeared I could still hear Joan's footsteps outside on the concrete floor of the verandah.

'Call yourself a wife? . . . Hello, old man! . . . Call yourself a wife?'

Then Joan had come in and had rushed across to me. Her eyes were sparkling. I'm afraid I wasn't very responsive after all that had happened. How I wished it hadn't! I'd never seen Jo look at me like that before.

'Hey, break away, you two! Now I ask you,' he turned to me,

'what do you think this woman who promised to love and cherish me . . .'

'Get on with it, Phil. Remember I haven't seen him for ever so long.' She looked up at me. There was no mistaking that look. She really was glad to see me. More than glad, it looked like. I could feel myself going all wobbly inside. If only . . .

'Well, here it is. We go to the pictures . . .' He broke off, turned and pointed an accusing finger at Jean. 'Did you use the car today, woman? I knew it, I knew it. We go to the pictures, I say, and, by the way, I agree with you for once, Jee, that Dean man doesn't bear repetition . . .'

'He does, he does, he's wonderful,' Joan interrupted, hugging me close, 'he's almost as nice as . . . as you, darling.'

My head was in a whirl.

'After the picture we come out, get in the car, start up for home, then at the bottom of the hill . . . phut, phut . . . no gas! A wife indeed! Don't you think you might have told me . . .'

'And what did you do?'

I could see Jean's hands clenched. The knuckles shone white.

'Do? Just sat there and waited till someone chose to come along and help us push it to the station. And what does this idiot sister of yours do but upbraid me for not remembering till then to tell her . . .'

'He never told me you were coming this evening. You knew I couldn't have got the message.'

'You've got him now, haven't you?'

'As if I'd have done you that! Not even for Malory Dean.'

Jo darling!

'And there I had to sit and listen to her . . . What must *he* be thinking of her? Did I think he'd be waiting? And then she just sat there and wouldn't say a word. Looking like a stuffed owl. "What are you thinking of?" I asked her. "I want to see *him*," was all she'd say.'

I saw Jean's hands relax. What a sigh she gave! A wonder the others didn't notice it. She turned, looked over at me and smiled. Her eyes shone.

'And at last two hefty chaps came along and helped us push.

And that reminds me. Four bob stopped out of your allowance next month and I've gone and strained a muscle in my leg . . .'

'Poor darling. Oh, I'm so sorry, Phil; you'll never know how sorry . . .' Her voice trailed away as she snuggled close in his arms.

'Let's leave the love-birds,' said Joan, tugging me out on to the verandah. 'Besides . . .'

So Jee had listened in all right but had got a message not intended for Phil. I had no doubt now how she felt towards me. Why, . . .

(B)

Joan came in first. She held out a hand to me. 'Hello.'

There was a queer catch in her breath as if she'd been running and her hand was cold and trembled in mine.

She turned away abruptly and crossed over to the window where she stood looking out into the night.

'Where's Phil?' asked Jean.

'Closing the garage,' she replied without looking around. Her fingers were drumming on the window-sill.

There was an uncomfortable pause. I was about to make a move to leave, but Jean motioned me to remain where I was. We all stood there motionless.

At last Joan turned. 'There's something we've got to tell you.' Then to me, 'Would you mind . . .'

'I know. He knows too.'

Joan drew a long shuddering breath. 'You know . . . Yes, of course you would know. I felt it. Like that horrible dream . . .'

She sank into a chair and covered her face with her hands. Jean went over to her.

'Jo, darling Jo!'

'Jee!'

'Don't cry . . .'

'I'm such a beast, Jee. How can you ever forgive me? But you must, you must . . . And Phil . . . you mustn't blame him. It's you he loves. I know now. And I . . .'

I met Phil on the verandah.

'Hello, Phil. Guess I'll be buzzing off.'

He made no reply but went in.

A voice, Jean's, called, 'Don't go. Wait, please wait.'

Then the door was pulled to.

So I sat on the balustrade and waited. Waited and smoked. Couldn't think of anything in particular except the twins crying on each other's shoulders. I'd seen them like that so often. Two little children crying. God, how the years fly!

I don't know how long I sat there. It might have been hours: it felt so. At last the door opened and Jean came out.

She handed me her suitcase.

'Sorry, but you'll have to walk over to Mother's with me.'

Joan appeared in the doorway.

'Look after her, please.'

And so I did. In fact I still do.

Some People Are Meant to Live Alone

Some people are meant to live alone. Take, for instance, Uncle Arthur. We called him Uncle Arthur, all of us, but he wasn't our uncle. He was really some sort of elderly cousin and he was almost a legend in the family. 'I'll send you to live with Uncle Arthur,' was Mother's threat when one of us had been particularly unruly, or 'A week with Uncle Arthur'll do you good.' Not that Uncle Arthur was especially ogre-like or repulsive to our childish eyes. Far from it – a milder little man I never saw, although his visits to our home in those days were few and far between. No, it was the fact that he lived all alone; alone in the old, dilapidated house on the hill, a house we could see when the canes were cut, a house that loomed gaunt and cockeyed against the brooding background of the two huge twisted evergreens that added their touch of mystery to his unaccountable isolation. None of us had ever been there. Uncle Arthur never invited anyone to his home. So the threat of being sent to Uncle Arthur's never lost its sting, even though at Christmas time we could always expect a large, clumsily wrapped box of toffee or butterscotch from the house on the hill.

Uncle Arthur's visits grew fewer and fewer till there was no in between, and it wasn't till I'd grown up that I ever gave him a thought again.

I was convalescing from an attack of 'flu, and I must have been a bit curt in replying to Mother who was fussing around my room before wishing me goodnight.

'Naughty boy, I think a week at Uncle Arthur's is what you really want.'

'A week at Uncle Arthur's!' What childhood memories the old phrase brought back.

'By the way, Mother,' I asked, 'whatever is the mystery about the old man?'

'Mystery! I really can't say there was ever any mystery. He's just one of those unfortunate souls that can't manage to live with anybody.'

'Why not?'

Mother, only too glad of an excuse to remain a little longer, sat at the foot of my bed.

'Well, he got married when he was quite young. They lived rather a cat and dog life. Eventually she disappeared. Ran off with a travelling agent, I believe. She wasn't much good, anyway. Fortunately there weren't any children. Then . . . well, I'm afraid he grew too fond of his cook. Then *she* skedaddled one day with most of the spare cash. It was quite a scandal. After that I suppose he decided to remain a bachelor. From time to time one or other of his sisters went to keep house for him, but none of them stayed very long. Then an old school friend appeared on the scene. They seemed to get on very well together. Might have been a couple of years. Then the friend . . . another of life's failures, he was . . . got drowned. People said it was suicide. Since then Uncle Arthur has lived by himself.'

'How long ago was that?'

'That was the year you had the mumps. Dear me, how time flies!'

'How old is he now?'

'Let me see.' Mother did a bit of complicated calculation on her fingers. 'Nineteen sixteen. Ethel died in nineteen o two. About sixty, I should think.'

'Good Lord, he looked that when I last saw him. And that was years ago.'

'Yes, he aged rather early, poor dear.'

'But whatever does he do up there all by himself?'

'Oh, he has an old woman to cook his meals. And he reads a great deal. And he's interested in painting, I think.'

'Have you ever been there?'

'Have I ever been there? Why, I was born there, silly. But I haven't been there since . . . since that business with the cook. I

often wonder what the old place looks like now. I hear the carriage house has completely tumbled down . . .'

We didn't talk any more about Uncle Arthur, but that night I dreamt of him. One of those long, rambling dreams you have when you're convalescing. Uncle Arthur showing me his paintings. They were all done on the ceiling, and I had to lie on the dining-table to look at them. I couldn't get him out of my mind for the next few days. As soon as I was up and about I decided I'd pay him a visit. It wasn't more than three miles away up the short cut by the hill, so I strolled over one afternoon.

Climbing up the hill was harder going than I'd thought. I hadn't quite got back into the swing of living yet. I sat on the guard-wall at the entrance and had a look at the old house. It was an old-fashioned two-storeyed building with a low open verandah facing the road. The evergreens on either side of the doorway merged their bushy branches overhead so that the upper storey was hardly visible. All the doors and windows I could see were closed. A white cat lay curled on the verandah.

Why on earth had I come? Perhaps it was the books, perhaps because I too happened to be interested in painting. I didn't know. Well, here I was. I rose to my feet and approached the house. Beneath the evergreens was moss-grown and damp, and although it couldn't have been later than five, whistling frogs were tuning up. The cat rose as I approached and stretched herself encouragingly. I mounted the weather-worn steps, knocked at the door and stroked her. She looked remarkably well-fed and contented. I waited a few moments and then knocked again. Presently I was aware of two eyes peering at me through a broken flap of the jalousies. I pretended not to notice and turned so that the afternoon sun might show me up more clearly. After a brief interval I heard a key turn in the lock and the door grated open. Though I hadn't seen him for so many years I recognised him at once. He didn't seem to have changed at all. He was barefooted and was wearing a pair of old flannels and a faded pyjama jacket. His untidy grey hair fell about his forehead just as it always did, and his meek, rather plaintive features were screwed up into an unasked question.

'Hello, Uncle Arthur! It's Bill. I don't suppose you remember me.'

'Bill . . . Bill . . .' His eyes blinked and he frowned. 'I'm sorry, but I'm afraid you've got the better of me.'

'I'm Bill . . . Bill Church.'

'You mean . . . you mean you're Rosie's son? Come in, come in! I *am* glad to see you. Well, well, I'd never have recognised you.'

I followed him through a very cheerless looking hallway and up a rickety flight of stairs.

'Careful, son. I don't use this part of the house very much. Mind out . . . that one's missing. Well, here we are.'

I was altogether surprised on entering the room at the top of the stairs. But for a large table littered with a miscellany of papers, books, cardboard boxes and empty cigarette tins in its further corner, the room was well furnished and comparatively tidy. Low bookshelves skirted the walls; there were a couple of comfortable armchairs and a divan, a rug that had seen better days but which was still full of warm colour, and an up-to-date Victrola with stacks of records. The late afternoon sunlight struggled through the evergreen branches that almost thrust themselves into the room and lit up the two pictures that hung over the largest of the bookshelves.

Uncle Arthur watched me closely as I took my bearings.

'Like it?'

'I should say. Why, this is what I always thought a room should be.'

Uncle Arthur grinned. I noticed for the first time that his face took on an impish, delightfully humorous expression when he smiled. I felt thoroughly at ease.

'Did you paint those?'

'Those? Dear me, no . . . That one's a Cézanne, the other a Gauguin. Reproductions, of course . . . German . . . but aren't they exquisite?'

Well, he started off on painting . . . Impressionism, the Pre-Raphaelites, the Post-Impressionists . . . Though I didn't understand half of what he was trying to tell me, I found it all fascinating. By degrees I discovered he'd done some painting himself, but he wouldn't show me any of his pictures. He gave me the impression of being extremely shy and sensitive. He went on to make excuses for the shabbiness of the house. He intended doing something . . . sometime. Of course he remembered Mother as a little girl. In fact, this had been her bedroom in the old days. He recalled how one day he had been summoned to make her come in off the roof. 'I'm afraid it wouldn't hold her up now,' he added ruefully. 'I mean, if she was still a little girl.' I laughed. Mother's size was a family joke.

We talked of all sorts of things. He played some records for me, a Beethoven concerto, and while I listened he brought in a decanter of rum and we had a couple of drinks. 'You must stay on and have pot luck. Tell you what I'll do: I'll send the cook's boy over to your mother's so she won't be anxious. There'll be a lovely moon to light your way down the hill.'

I stayed on. We ate at an old claw-footed mahogany table in the adjoining room, and the cook, an agreeable but unusually deaf old soul, served us. She wore brass ear-rings and a large floppy straw hat. The dinner was quite good, and after a great deal of shouting and gesticulation on Uncle Arthur's part, she brought in a liqueur which he served in cracked pony-glasses. Afterwards we returned to the living room. The moon, round and full, flooded the room with light. 'Shall I switch on, or is this good enough?'

'It's good enough,' I replied. I felt unusually serene and happy. The moonlight fell in a broad cool band across the rug, and a gentle breeze supplied a final touch of satisfaction to the scene.

'You know, I almost envy you, Uncle Arthur.' I was feeling particularly grown up . . . the rum and the liqueur, I suppose . . . and now, watching the blue haze of my cigarette smoke curling away mysteriously into the dim shadows of the room, I felt as though Uncle Arthur and I were two pals together. There was a singular charm and lightness of heart about the old man that appealed to me. The things he liked and talked about . . . music, painting, whimsical anecdotes of this and that . . . struck a responsive chord somewhere in me. Everybody I'd ever talked to was so confoundedly practical. As I sat there I wondered . . . perhaps some day I, like Uncle Arthur, might come to find a life like this all satisfying . . . Who could tell?

'Uncle Arthur, are you ever lonely? Really lonely, I mean?'

The old man sighed. 'No. I don't think so. Not really, honest to God lonely. No, I can't say that. Some people are meant to live alone. I'm one of them, I guess.' He paused and lit a cigarette. 'I'm really much happier when I'm alone.'

I thought of Betty, of football, of next week's dance . . . 'I wonder!'

'When you're young perhaps, no. But later on . . . Well . . .' He sighed again. 'I've tried both ways. I don't think I've ever been really happy with anyone for long. No. I prefer it this way.'

He was silent for a while. Suddenly I was overwhelmed by a feeling of intense affection for the old man. I resolved this was to be the first of many evenings in his company. I felt I was somehow on the threshold of a different existence, far more exciting, far more real than the sort I'd led; and I felt that despite all he'd said, he wasn't averse to my company.

'I knew a man once . . .' he began, then broke off. 'But I'm not good at telling stories.'

'Please!'

'It will only show you what some people will do to . . . Yes, some people are meant to live alone. This man . . . I'll call him Jones . . .' He broke off and chuckled. 'You know, it might be my own story. Ah well . . . Jones, when my story begins, had been married four or five years and he was desperately unhappy. His wife was one of the nagging sort. And a passion for doing this and doing that when this was finished. No sooner had poor Jones finished tidying up the garden beds than the furniture had to be polished. You know the type, I expect?'

I nodded with all the sagacity of my twenty-two years.

'And then one day she left him . . . or he left her . . . I'm not rightly sure which, but he was free, free to do as he liked. He decided marriage wasn't meant for him. No, sir. He could do just as he pleased. No wife to nag him, no people dropping in to talk and talk when he wanted to be left alone, nobody to remind him of what he had to do, what he ought to do, what he must do. It was delightful. He was irresponsible, gay, free. And then one day a dreadful thing happened. An old school chum of his turned up. Let's call him Smith. Smith was one of those unfortunate people who aren't satisfied unless they're *doing* things . . . dancing somewhere, eating somewhere, making love to someone, and so unhappy if left up to their own resources for five minutes, they begin to disintegrate. It so happened he'd done a little too much. First he'd helped himself to somebody else's money . . . that was smoothed over. Then he was arrested for murder. They hadn't enough evidence to convict him, but he was *fini*. Disowned by all his former friends, he could go nowhere, do nothing. The shock and the scandal had killed his poor old mother. He was desperate. He sought out his old friend, Jones. Would he let him stay with him? He was frantic. If only he had someone to keep him company . . . Jones was rather a sympathetic sort; besides, he didn't have the guts to say no. So Smith came to stay.

'At first it wasn't so bad. Smith was so glad to feel he wasn't altogether an outcast, he was fairly agreeable. That is to say, he kept out of Jones's way most of the time. At dinner he was apt to be rather a nuisance talking of what he'd done from time to time at cricket or football or some such, and then sometimes he'd drink a bit too much. And now that he couldn't go around with the society girls, he discovered that the girls in the village were quite flattered by his advances. Jones didn't mind: Smith's way of life was Smith's. But then unfortunately Smith went one night, for want of something to do, and poked his silly head into a revivalist tent and got his soul saved. Let me tell you, sonny, there's nothing worse than living in a house with a saved soul, that is, if it happens to be one like Smith's. Smith's soul gave him no rest. It was always reminding him of all his past sins. Now that was all right as far as Smith was concerned, but when Smith's soul began worrying about Jones's, then the trouble started.

'Smith would come in on Sundays all dressed up from prayer meeting and looking as though he'd had a personal interview with Old Nick, and find Jones in his shirt sleeves, a rum and ginger at his elbow, smoking his pipe and reading. He'd just sit and look at him and groan. After a while he'd go upstairs and then he'd begin to pray. Pray aloud. Jones told me that of all the things on earth that are likely to rouse thoughts of murder in a man's heart, there is nothing to equal the sound of a voice you do not particularly care for, praying on your behalf. After two or three Sundays of this Jones couldn't stand it any longer. He told him he'd either have to quit praying or quit the house. He'd been there well over a year; his soul was saved. Knowing that, he could now start life afresh.'

Uncle Arthur paused to hunt for his cigarette tin.

'And did he?'

'Not much. Smith cried like a child. He couldn't, he couldn't go and live somewhere all by himself. And then . . . then he confessed to having committed that murder. He couldn't live alone with the knowledge of that. If he woke in the night and felt there was nobody near him, nobody he really knew, he was certain he'd either go mad or kill himself. Would you believe it, he actually swore he'd never go to another prayer meeting if only Jones would let him stay. So again Jones gave way to his better and more cowardly feelings.'

He paused to light up.

'Wasn't he afraid Jones might tell on him?'

'If he did, that fear was overwhelmed by a far greater fear . . . the fear of being alone. He just couldn't come to terms with the reality of loneliness, the essential loneliness of humanity.

'So Smith stayed on. He didn't worry so much about his soul now. He seemed to have only one aim in life . . . to show Jones how much he appreciated his kindness in allowing him to stay on. Jones would be reading or writing or trying to doze off or something or other, and he'd be conscious that Smith was watching him. Not with any evil intent, you know. No, just watching him with a sort of dog-like devotion. It was embarrassing. It was horrible. Sometimes Jones would lose his temper and ask him for God's sake to leave him alone, and off he'd go meekly enough. And of an evening, after dinner, when Jones wanted to read and enjoy a pipe, Smith would walk up and down, up and down, just outside the window, solemn and silent, for all the world just like some Praetorian guard. It's an awful thing to listen to anyone pacing up and down like that. The confounded monotony of the thing, the soullessness of it, eats into your very core.

'One evening Jones couldn't stand it any longer. "God damn it, Smith," he said, "I can't stand this any longer. You've got to get out of here or I won't be responsible. You've got to go. First thing tomorrow morning. If you can't live alone, why don't you get married or something? Go and live with a woman. I'll give you the money. Any one of the girls in the village . . ." But Smith shrieked in horror and ran off. When Jones went to bed he hadn't yet returned. Jones went to sleep. In the middle of the night he woke and heard him in his room which was next door. He was praying again, praying earnestly and loudly that the soul of his dear friend, Jones, might be washed clean of all such lewd and sinful thoughts. Over and over, over and over the voice went on.

'Jones was a very quiet little fellow . . . I knew him well . . . but he told me something just went off pop inside him. He got up and went straight into Smith's room and strangled him.'

'He what?'

'Strangled him.'

'You mean, he murdered him?'

'Yes. He murdered him. He was sorry afterwards, of course, but he couldn't undo what he'd done.

'Well, poor Jones was in a very awkward position. He had to move and move quickly. In those days he had a car . . . it was the day of the old "upstairs" Ford, so he managed to haul the body downstairs and prop it up somehow in the car. It was two or three o'clock in the morning and there wasn't a soul stirring. Jones drove down to the cliff by Threecorner and dropped Smith overboard.'

'They never found the body?' I had suddenly gone very cold.

'About a week after. The fish had got at it. It was identified. Indeed I was one of the persons who identified it.'

I had to say it. I don't know why. 'And . . . and nobody ever suspected you, Uncle Arthur?'

He sighed. 'I told you I wasn't much good at telling a story. Ah well, I suppose I had to tell somebody sometime. Strange, you know, I've never felt the slightest twinge of conscience. I'd do exactly the same tomorrow in such circumstances. Only it didn't seem fair that nobody should know.'

I rose and switched on the light.

'Do you think you've been fair to me to tell me this?'

'Sorry, son. Perhaps not. But I don't know. I took a liking to you the moment I saw you through the jalousies. And I wanted to see you again. And I didn't want you to be under any misapprehensions as regards my character. But I see it's no go. Some people are meant to live alone. I will show you down the stairs. The moon's high now and you can get down the cliff easily.'

I couldn't say a word; I followed him down the stairs and with a mumbled goodbye I left him.

I never saw him again. The next year I proposed to Betty and we got married shortly afterwards. Our marriage was a failure from the first. Last year we got our divorce. And a week ago old Uncle Arthur died. He has left me his sole heir. He had some money. I think I shall repair the old house and go and live there. The thought fascinates me.

Some people, I suppose, are meant to live alone.

Release

The two men leaned against the wall opposite. Their bodies, slack, inanimate, would have conveyed no significance to the casual passer-by, but to him, pausing there in the twist of the alley, those slouching forms were symbols of desperation. But he could not turn back now. Behind him the light of the street-lamp stabbed the cobblestones with a thousand spearheads: out there in the street they were waiting for him.

'You boys stand here. He may have gone down the alley. Wait . . . wait all night if necessary.'

Should he go on? Maybe they were only two drunks. His breath was hot and panting. Screwed tight in his heart, hope flamed and died away again. 'They've got you, son, they've got you this time.' He'd always known this would happen. Authority with its thugs and guns always got you. No use now to harken back to those smooth, slimy words that had so nearly clogged his will once. He had made his choice. Either a place at the board of the oppressors or this. Hunted, snared. He'd made his choice. Life was no good with eyes and ears closed, heart shut to justice and the claims of humanity.

Sweating, panting, he watched the two forms there. So inane, so removed from the stir, the violence of life. Shall I pass? Beyond them, the river. The river, cold under the stars. If not, another coldness, the coldness of death.

Was it for this he had been born into the world, a stranger learning its harsh lessons until now? Learning the bitter realisation of the power of injustice, the seething contempt for authority, an authority which could place fetters upon the message of the mind and the spirit, upon the undying heritage of man?

He must control that bursting breath, that pulse that tolled his doom to wary ears. The two forms stood silent; but would they not hear his heart? Overhead in the narrow strip of sky beyond the lowering roof-tops the patterned stars offered no counsel. Grave and dispassionate, they blinked at him unseeingly through the cold inter-stellar space. He would have liked to pray, but his schooling had robbed him of that refuge, pricked the bubble of his childish dreams. Out there hung only the ghost of jejune fantasy. The moments knew no pause.

He straightened himself. In this dark labyrinth evil triumphed. Lend thy likeness to evil.

He skewed the cap over his eyes. No one would notice a lonely drunk. Drunk to the world, lost in the sottishness of its own misapprehension. Reel and lurch across the stones. This aping of the degradation of humanity might lead to freedom, past these silent symbols of fear.

He staggered forward.

The figures made no movement.

Twenty, fifteen, ten feet away. His lurching feet wove a crazy pathway over the stones. Even so did the rulers spurn the good earth from which men's bodies were fashioned.

One of them wore boots that were burst where the uppers joined the soles. There were dark stains on the unpolished leather. The other wore shoes, jaunty patent-leather shoes, shining in the starlight, shining with the fires of hell.

He stumbled on. Only his hope, his beating hope had eyes, but the eyes, even those eyes, were glazed with fear.

Five paces off. Four. Three. Two.

Puppets. Hung by unseen wires from the void. A string was pulled. The patent-leather shoes moved. The puppets came to life.

'Not so fast, brother.'

He made no sign. He would pass them. This, this only the answer. He staggered on. To stagger, chanceler. Chanceler Chanticleer . . .

> While the cock with lively din
> Scatters the rear of darkness thin . . .

Thin! No. Thick blinding darkness, the darkness that would not, could not comprehend. And the light shone in the darkness . . .

The hand fell upon his shoulder. The patent-leather shoes formed the centre of his vision.

'Cut it out. We got your number.'

He would not speak. Not to these, these, the scum of darkness. Two pairs of feet, one in trim, pointed patent-leather shoes, the other in blunt, broken boots.

The hand shook him roughly. He could not see, but he could sense the cold merciless metal of revolvers near. He tried to raise a hand, to pass it over his mouth in drunken gesture as he'd often seen it done; but the hand, both his hands, were in vices of hot, hard flesh.

He spat weakly, slobberingly upon the ground.

'Game's up, I tell you.'

A shoe, delicately pointed, raised itself and descended viciously upon his instep. He winced and within him something moaned. No . . . no . . . not that weakness of the flesh corrupting the other courage. Let that not fall, that lonely barrier against the body's weakness. He bit his lip in despair.

The other voice spoke. God, that boots should have voices! It spoke smoothly with a refined accent. He noticed the boots were old, but they had seen better days.

'There's no possible use in pretending to be drunk. We've got you this time.'

It was pressed there in his back. Hard, impersonal. He shifted his stance but the muzzle followed him. It was bound to him now, he knew, a part of him for ever.

'You've got a chance, you know.'

It had come at last. This, the final agony. Dear light, that shone in the fields over swaying grasses, that played upon the dancing waters, that in the last brief hours of day gathered its robe of cloud into the shining west, dear light of the world, let not this come to pass! Grant him one last, one only mercy! Not this, not this, the soul's final abasement.

'Tell us where the meeting-place is and we shall spare you.'

'Life is sweet, brother,' coaxed the patent-leather shoes.

Something warm ran down his chin. Hold fast, my lips, hold . . .

'All you need do is say the word. You shall find us not unmindful of services rendered. This is no way to die.'

He closed his eyes. Faces of comrades swayed up to him. Smiling . . . sad . . . they swayed up to him out of the darkness, and, since his hands were bound, kissed him on the brow. One of them, a pale, slim girl, caught the blood that dripped from his lip in her cupped hands and bent her head in compassion with closed eyes. Then she kissed him on the mouth. He could give them their liberty now, his coward lips. Through them his freed soul spoke:

'Shoot! Shoot and be damned to you.'

The broken boots and the finicking shining shoes still bounded his horizon. But he would not go down into the darkness with their hideousness engraven upon his mind. Nor would he look at their faces. He wanted no more hatred to quicken within him now. He raised his head. Up there, up there in the sky there was still light. Beauty still lived on.

A faint breeze blew down the alley. Out there, beyond the city, trees still rustled in the night wind, and the grass would shine green when the night was gone.

The sound of the revolver shot was dulled in the folds of his loose-fitting coat. Overhead the stars rocketed into a great gulf of blackness.

Second Attempt

Mrs Rinfer gave the flowers in the blue bowl a final little pat and stepped back to survey the effect. There now, that was delightful! So were the curtains. She had chosen the stuff for the curtains herself and had put them up that very morning. But the furniture left much to be desired. Why did people put such uncomfortable chairs in their drawing rooms? Even the cushions on the divan were lumpy. The pictures, however, were not too outrageous, and there was something rather pathetic about the long mirror in its tarnished gilt frame.

Crossing the room she surveyed her reflection in it and gave a wisp of hair that had got loose a reproving twiddle. Astonishing how her hair had kept its colour so well. She turned sideways. Holding herself in like that she didn't look too plump; that is, not for a widow of forty-three. And *he* would soon be here. Twenty-four years! Why, it seemed only like yesterday. She glanced at the clock in the adjoining room. A quarter to six. He should be here at any moment now. What a blessed invention cocktails were! She couldn't very well have asked him for dinner . . . at least, not yet. She wondered how he would react to his being the only guest; but then she had that story about the Browns all arranged. And then, with a sudden little pang of anxiety, she wondered, 'Will he have changed much?' Twenty-four years was a long time, after all. He'd been rather a good-looking young man. He would be nearly fifty now. When she'd phoned him his voice had sounded much the same as she'd remembered it. And the catch in his breath as he'd said, 'Mu . . . riel!' Well, she hadn't been forgotten. She hoped he hadn't gone bald: that would be worse than if he'd put on too much weight. But it wasn't any good burning one's bridges before one came to them . . . That didn't seem quite right, but she knew what she meant.

'Everything ready, Millicent?' she called out to the maid.

'Yes'm,' Millicent replied.

Thank God, she could leave all the preparations to Millicent. Sandwiches, stuffed eggs, the cocktails . . . Millicent could be depended upon for everything. And she had a marvellous sense of timing; she knew just when to appear with the necessary refreshment.

Raindrops pattered on the window-pane. She hurried over to the window and scanned the sky anxiously. A swarthy cloud squatted directly overhead. It would be awful if it began to fall hard just now!

Footsteps on the verandah made her swing around. It was, it was James.

'James!' She almost tripped on the rug in her anxiety to reach him, to make him feel he was welcome.

'How are you, Mu-Muriel?' He came forward shyly and grasped her outstretched hand.

She fussed about him delightedly. 'It's grand to see you again.'

Standing there in the doorway against the late afternoon glow he looked quite slim and boyish; now sitting there beside him she could see how he had changed. His face was much too thin, the high cheekbones much too prominent, there were too many lines on the forehead, the creases at the corners of the mouth too pronounced, the grey eyes behind the thick lenses of his gold-rimmed glasses too sad, the once brown hair too faded and greyish . . . but he wasn't bald, thank God.

He was very silent as he sat there watching her. But that wasn't anything new.

She broke the silence.

'Dear James,' she heard herself saying.

A little smile played around the corners of his mouth. No, he hadn't changed so much after all.

'It . . . it seems I'm the first to get here.'

'I do hope you won't mind, but the Browns can't come; Esmée's gone and got the 'flu or something, and I really didn't want to put you off.'

He made no reply, so she rattled away. 'Some people simply can't be depended upon. Fancy her waiting till this afternoon . . .' She lied on cheerfully, charmingly. 'But in a way I'm not sorry,' she concluded, 'it's nice to meet you like this where we can talk over old times without fear of interruption.'

He smiled again. She'd always liked his smile. There was something rather sweet and disarming about it. A sudden thought struck her.

'But here I am chattering away and you must have got caught in that drizzle.' She leaned over and placed a plump hand on his coat sleeve. 'There, I thought so. And all this 'flu about, too. But we'll soon put that right.' She smiled roguishly and he noticed that her eyes crinkled at the corners as they'd always done. 'Millicent! . . . There's nothing like a cocktail for warding off the 'flu.'

'I shouldn't mind.'

She watched him take a cocktail from the tray and fumble for a sandwich. How clumsy he is, she thought, the dear old thing.

'When did you arrive, Muriel?' He had got the sandwich at last.

'Last Friday. I was lucky to get a furnished place so soon, don't you think?'

He looked around non-committally.

'Um . . . hum . . .'

'Don't you like the curtains though? They're mine.'

He blinked at them approvingly.

'And how long are you here for, Muriel?'

Really! How could she answer him when everything depended on him? At least, on whether she could induce him to help her in settling the question of her future.

She looked pensively at the mixture in her glass.

'I don't know. You see, Jack left me none too well off, and I'm rather thinking of going to live with Nita . . . that's my sister-in-law. But I just had to come back to Barbados if only for a few weeks before settling down. It's not much fun living in Trinidad nowadays.'

She gave a little sigh, then smiled at him and raised her glass: 'Good luck!'

'Good luck!'

'Trinidad's not what it used to be, you know.'

'So they tell me.'

She told him the story everyone who lives in Trinidad tells everyone who doesn't. It took a little time.

After his third cocktail he admired the flowers. 'Gardening's my hobby, you know,' he said shyly.

'Really?'

'Yes.'

'But then you always loved flowers.'

He could see her now, slim and graceful, a little flushed as she clasped a profusion of white coralita to her bosom. Her eyes were shining. How beautiful she was! The wind played softly upon her and a wisp of her hair mingled with the delicate spray of coralita that twined itself above her head. He'd known her only a short while and he'd liked her, but it wasn't until that afternoon as she stood there clasping the wayward strands of coralita to her that he was overwhelmed by love for her. It was a Sunday, the Sunday after his father had died. He'd been so sad. Everything had seemed so hopeless . . . and then her beauty and his love for her breaking in upon him like a torrent. He had been a little ashamed of his happiness: it had seemed so unfair to his mother. He had come to life that day. And then . . . so soon after . . . he had died . . .

'You always loved flowers, didn't you?'

'Yes, indeed.' He toyed with the empty glass beside him.

Her heart went pit-a-pat. Dear James. What would it have been like, she thought, had she married him instead? She'd always liked him very much. At least he would have been more considerate than Jack. Jack, loud-voiced, brutal in his lack of sensibility. And his women . . . his awful women . . .

'And you never married, James?'

'Me?' He uttered a short nervous laugh. 'No, my dear. Marriage isn't for everyone.'

'Rubbish.'

'Not for me at any rate.'

'Why not? Here you are, a successful accountant, for years and years a kind devoted son . . .'

'What's that got to do with it?'

'What! A man who could give up all those years to looking after an invalid mother . . .'

He frowned. 'I'm not so sure of that. I only did my duty.'

'Exactly. Exactly. That's what I'm telling you. A sense of duty plays a part in marriage. A very important part.'

'It's not the same thing.'

'And you mean to say you never even had a love affair? Not even a teeny little one?'

He blushed. No, he hadn't changed one bit.

'You don't have to be modest about it, you know. Remember I'm an old married woman.'

Through the thick lenses the eyes looked larger and sadder than ever. She could read the sincerity of their mild reproach.

'You'll think me an awful simpleton, Muriel; but there's been nothing, absolutely nothing.'

'But why . . . why?'

He looked away. She could feel that the eyes were brimming with tears. Oh, she felt mean, mean. And at the same time profoundly touched.

She leaned over and placed a hand on his arm.

'I'm sorry, dear. I didn't mean to be inquisitive. Forgive me.'

He was about to pat the hand reassuringly, but the cocktail glass was in the way. He made a muffled noise of acknowledgement.

She mustn't let him think *she* had escaped.

'*My* married life wasn't exactly a success, you know.'

He turned quickly and she was startled and thrilled at the solicitude of his regard.

'My dear . . . I mean . . . I'm sorry. I . . . I was never quite sure.'

'Ah well, we won't discuss it. Millicent!'

They helped themselves to the cocktails. Silence had fallen upon them. He sipped his slowly, meditatively. He had loved her so. God, how he had loved her! As he thought of that time he could feel the memory of the old pang in his heart. He glanced at her. She too seemed lost in some memory of the past. He remembered that night. The last night he had seen her. How he had staked everything on it! What a ghastly failure it had been! That night when overcoming his cursed shyness he had . . . He shuddered at the memory of it. He must have made some little sound at the recollection, for she turned to him.

'Yes?'

'No. No. I didn't say anything.'

There was a pause. Why did this memory have to intrude itself upon him now? He looked at his watch. 'I think . . .'

'James dear, will you answer me one question?'

'Certainly . . . if I can.'

'I was wondering . . . I've often wondered . . . why did you never come back after that night?'

He was silent. She too had remembered that awful night. He didn't answer.

'Won't you tell me? Was it anything I did or said?'

'You! Of course not!' There was no mistaking the tone of shocked sincerity. 'How else could you have acted? The fault was mine.'

But she couldn't understand for the life of her what he was talking about.

He continued haltingly: 'I don't suppose you have ever forgiven me. I have never forgiven myself. For I insulted you. I . . . I outraged your . . . your essential innocence.' He hung his head.

She felt that the time had come to speak to him sharply.

'Now, James, we've got to get this thing straight. Would you mind if we ran through the events of that night?'

He made no response.

'Very well. I will. Stop me if I go wrong. You took me to the movies. It was Valentino in *The Four Horsemen*. Afterwards you suggested taking me for a drive. You drove me out to that quaint little old church by the sea . . .'

'St Basil.'

'St Basil. And we parked there for a while. You were particularly silent that night. Silent and ill at ease. Then suddenly you . . . you drove home again. You wouldn't even come in though Mother came to the door and asked you to; and then you drove off without as much as a goodnight to me. Do you realise this is the first time I've seen you since?'

So she was going to compel him to say what he'd done? Very

well, he would. At any rate, doing so might bring his conscience some relief.

'You know, Muriel, I was very inexperienced. You see, I . . . I respected womanhood. All womanhood. And you won't mind my saying so, but I . . . I worshipped you. Will you believe me when I tell you I'd sooner have cut off my right hand than to have done what I did?'

Her eyes were wide open with amazement. Whatever did the man mean?

'That night I'd decided I must tell you how much I loved you. I had it all planned out. I thought I'd ask you at some suitable moment to look up at the stars; then I thought I'd . . . I'd hold your hand and say: "They're beautiful, but not half as beautiful as you" . . . or something like that.' He broke off and ran his hands through his hair.

Wait! It was coming back to her from out there in the past . . . the breeze from the sea, Orion straddled across the old church steeple . . . a dog barking in the distance, and something . . . something unpleasant . . . what was it?

'So I did as I'd intended. And you looked up at the stars. And then . . . and then something went wrong inside me. I couldn't say anything. I . . . I just wanted to hold your beautiful body close to me. I threw my arms around you . . .'

It had all come back to her. 'Don't . . . don't say any more. I remember.'

But he couldn't stop now. He must make his confession. 'You broke away from me with a cry of disgust. I really hadn't intended being so impertinent . . . so fresh. I shall never forget that cry. It has haunted me. The cry of outraged virtue . . .' He closed his eyes. He could see her still, shrinking back from him, her eyes filled with unspeakable loathing.

He was afraid to look at her now after all these years.

But she said nothing and he turned to her. She was sobbing.

'Muriel, Muriel, can you forgive me?'

She looked up at him. And then he realised she wasn't sobbing. She was shaking . . . shaking with suppressed laughter!

He couldn't believe his eyes.

'What are you laughing at?'

'I'm . . . I'm sorry, darling. Oh, but . . . do let me explain.' She attempted to dry her eyes, but it was no good. She just couldn't stop laughing.

'Muriel!'

He was hurt. Hurt to the depths of his soul. To have confessed his shame to her, God knew with what agony of spirit, to have laid bare the secret that had spoilt his life . . . and then to be laughed at. He was bitterly, bitterly hurt.

'James, James, you poor darling . . . So that's what it was . . . that's what it was . . . if I'd only known! But, you see, it was only . . . only . . .'

The sight of the wounded expression of the sad grey eyes sobered her partially.

'. . . only a boil!'

'A boil?'

'Yes. You see, I had a large boil and it was so painful . . . right on my . . . under my arm, and when you threw your arms round me . . . my outraged virtue . . . oh, oh, oh!' She was off again.

He rose to his feet.

'I must be going.'

Collapsing on to the floor she clutched at his legs. 'No. No. Don't go.' She looked up at him. 'Don't you see . . . the irony of it, James? The irony? You and your dear old-fashioned notions of love, and me with my sense of maiden delicacy not wanting to let you know that your goddess suffered from anything so vulgar as a boil?'

A boil! The utter mockery of those wasted years!

Looking down at her crouching there on the faded rug, her body torn with uncontrollable sobs of laughter, a sudden wave of compassion surged up within him. Neither anger nor love mattered any more. Nothing mattered now. All the wasted years lay thick upon his soul, crushing it dry of all thoughts of self.

He raised her gently to her feet.

'Goodnight, Muriel. I'm sorry.'

She couldn't say anything.

'Goodbye.'

He turned and walked slowly through the door.

Her heart was numb. She would laugh and laugh when he was

safe out of hearing, laugh till all the tears and laughter in her were for ever one, complete and indivisible.

She threw herself on the divan.

She had plotted and planned to get him for herself since Jack died. Even when Jack was alive . . . And now all her plotting and planning were of no avail. How her sister-in-law would laugh at her! Widow's wiles foiled . . . foiled by a boil . . . Never mind, you must try somebody else, darling . . . Hell, she didn't want anybody else . . . she wanted . . . Suddenly she realised it all. She loved him. Loved him with all the good and all the bad in her. Had always loved him. And . . . and . . .

Like a mad woman she rushed out on the verandah. She'd run down the street after him. She'd . . .

He was standing there in the semi-darkness of the verandah looking up into the sky. He made no movement. She went up to him slowly and placed a trembling hand upon his shoulder.

He turned to her and looked into her eyes gravely.

'Look up at the stars, darling.'

'You . . . you don't have to tell me they're not half so beautiful as I am . . . now . . .'

'No, perhaps not. But there's one thing I want to ask you.'

'Yes . . . yes . . .?'

'You haven't got any boils now . . . anywhere, have you, sweet?'

There's Always the Angels

'Have you ever been a god?'

It was with difficulty that I murmured a perfunctory 'I beg your pardon?' to the old gentleman who was occupying the seat on the park bench beside me. I'd certainly never been asked that question before.

He repeated it, a faintly humorous smile playing about his lips as he did so; but his large brown eyes were very sad.

'Why, no,' I replied after another moment of hesitation.

He eyed me thoughtfully, critically, as though he was making up his mind about something. Then he spoke again with a little sigh, wistfully, as though making a confession of something he wasn't too proud of. 'I have, you know.'

'Oh!' I said. It didn't mean anything, but then what else could I have said?

'Yes,' he repeated slowly, 'I have.'

He sat there lost in meditation looking over across the trim lawn to where against a background of dim mahogany trees a couple, a young man and a girl, were pacing slowly, arm in arm, up and down.

I looked at him closely for the first time. I hadn't paid him much attention when I'd taken my seat. Indeed, I'd thought at first he was a clergyman, one of those elderly retired clergymen you see taking an evening stroll, sitting in the park for a few moments before, refreshed by the sight of the trees and flowers, they move on slowly homewards, ere it grows dark. But on closer inspection I decided he wasn't a clergyman. He wasn't dressed like a clergyman. His clothes, a bit shabby, had nothing suggestive of the clerical about them. And he wore a very bright blue tie that was in some way . . . An artist, that's what he was. The tie, those long tapering fingers. Musician, painter? I stole a glance at his face now in profile. It must have been a very handsome face once, I thought. Even now, despite the many wrinkles and a slight grey stubble, it was worthwhile looking at. There was a peculiar air of aloofness about its expression, a sort of brooding absorption. The sort of face . . . Ah, I was sure now: a scientist.

'Pardon me,' I began, but at that moment he turned and addressed me again.

'Life. Life on this planet of ours. It's not what it ought to be, you know. Don't you find it very confusing?'

I was about to reply but he continued:

'Yes, you must have given the matter some consideration. It's inevitable. It all could be so pleasant. So very pleasant.'

He broke off again. He spoke in jerks, but smooth little jerks, if you know what I mean.

'Over there. That boy and girl. In love and planning for happiness. And what? A background of pain and evil and disease and death. And war. Always war. Always evil. Why?'

I replied to the effect that I supposed it was in the nature of things.

'But surely it oughtn't to be in the nature of things. It wasn't intended. I know it wasn't. I . . .' He ran a hand through his thinning greyish hair.

'Yes?'

'You see, knowing this, I thought: Why not make another universe, a universe I could control. A universe from which pain and violence and evil would be excluded. Where there'd be only life and joy and happiness. You understand?'

'Quite. Only it's . . . well, it's not so easy, creating a universe, is it?'

He took me up rather sharply. 'That depends, my dear fellow, that depends.'

'Upon what?'

'This universe as you know it, what is it really? I will tell you. It is a thought in the mind of the one who created it, of God. Now I ask you, can't you draw the inference?'

'Well, I suppose anybody could *think* out a universe, if that's what you mean,' I replied cautiously. 'But I shouldn't imagine it would be a very real sort of universe.'

'That's where you're utterly mistaken.' He was rather heated now. 'I admit it isn't very easy, but it can be done. I tell you I know what I'm talking about. Because I've done it.'

Again I ventured a non-committal 'Oh!'

He was looking out now, over the tops of the darkened mahogany trees, into the late afternoon glow of the sunset, and there was a sort of nobility about the face that touched me.

'At first, you know, there was chaos. Confusion. Nothing and everything. It's difficult to think of everything. But it's more difficult to think of nothing. Have you ever tried thinking of nothing?'

But he didn't seem to be expecting any answer and he went on:

'Yes, it was all terribly difficult at the beginning. But at last I felt I could begin. It was all here.' He tapped his forehead. 'All here in the same way . . .'

He broke off again. He seemed to be thinking of something else.

'In the same way . . .' I prompted.

'Let's not talk of that now,' he said. 'As I was saying, I began again.'

'Again?'

'One must experiment, you know. I wanted this universe of mine, this new universe, if I may put it that way, to be perfect. Well, I began in the orthodox manner. Light first. It's funny, but it's got to be so. I suppose you've often wondered about that part of the biblical story. Light first, sun and so on afterwards. But it's really so. You try it if you don't believe me. Yes, the first thing has got to be light. So I began. I worked on the approved model. I shan't tire you with a detailed description, of course. Only I did want to have a moon all the year round.'

'And why didn't you?'

'No. I couldn't forgo the starlight. And then, you can't improve upon the stars, can you?'

I made no comment.

'And so I went on and on. I thought of introducing a few new varieties of plant life, but somehow . . . And it was delightful creating the birds.'

'Did they prey upon one another?' I ventured.

But he didn't reply. He went on. 'And so, at last, I came to the final creation, man.'

'With or without appendix?' You see, I was just convalescing from the operation.

But he ignored that question too.

'My masterpiece.'

'What did he look like?'

This time he replied. 'Well, he was rather like . . . like me. Me, but much younger, of course. I wasn't a bad-looking young man. But that was long ago. However. Still I wasn't satisfied: so I created a partner for him. A woman.'

'Rib?'

His answer led me to think he was a little hard of hearing.

'Never mind about the name. But she was very beautiful. And they were happy in the garden. Very happy. And I thought: Now this is where things went wrong in the other garden. So I didn't put any restrictions upon them. No tree. No inhibitions. I felt I was wiser. I'd read Freud in the meantime. And then . . . and then . . .'

He broke off and buried his face in his hands. I had a suspicion he was sobbing, sobbing very quietly.

After a suitable pause I coughed. It was getting late.

He looked up. His eyes *were* wet.

'And then . . .' I reminded him.

'I don't know.'

'You don't know?'

He shook his head sadly. 'No. I don't think I shall ever know.'

There was something so hopeless in the tone of these words that suddenly I was filled with an overwhelming wave of pity for the old fellow. I looked away. I couldn't bear to think this fantasy of his could have such an effect upon him. A tall man was walking slowly in our direction. A man in a tweed suit and a felt hat. I could barely distinguish it was a tweed suit in the gathering darkness.

'I don't *want* to know. I don't *want* to know.' He was clutching me by the arm.

I gave his hand a reassuring pressure.

'I don't *want* to know, I tell you.' He was sobbing now unashamedly.

I squeezed his hand again. 'Oh, it's sure to be all right,' I said. 'After all, you made your little universe; you can make things go how you want them to.'

'But that's the awful part,' he moaned. 'Look at what's happening to the one you're living in.'

'But,' I began smilingly.

The man in the tweed suit had come alongside us and touched his shabby felt hat to us.

'Good-evening,' I returned.

The old gentleman didn't notice him. He withdrew his hand and looked at me intently. There was something extremely disconcerting in his regard. 'You see, I made the one you're living in also.'

The man in the tweed suit smiled at me not unsympathetically, and touched the old gentleman on the shoulder.

'Come along, sir. Nearly seven o'clock, you know.'

'Yes, I know, Michael.'

He rose, wiped his eyes on a faded silk handkerchief and blew his nose softly.

'Good-evening,' he said to me. 'Must be off.' He patted the man affectionately on the shoulder. 'After all, there's always the angels.' And he gave me a knowing wink.

They moved away. The lovers had long since departed. The park bell rang for closing time.

Good Lord, I thought, what a sad case! And such a nice old fellow too! And I hadn't even discovered who he was. At least, I could have asked the keeper his name.

I got up and tried to overtake them. But it was no good; I couldn't walk very quickly. When I reached the gate they had disappeared. I made enquiries about them afterwards, but strangely enough, I've never been able to trace them.

Mr Baker Forgets Himself

Enclosed within the impervious walls of self, Laureston Baker, you might have thought, would have never been able to perform an act which demanded self-abnegation and a certain amount of courage. And no one could have blamed you for entertaining such a thought. Indeed, it was precisely this thought that was worrying him on the evening of which I write.

Beyond the fact that he was an accountant and a widower of some twenty years' standing, little else was known of Laureston Baker. He was not the sort of man that invited confidences and friendship. No one knew him intimately; indeed, the only person who had some grounds for believing he had that knowledge was himself. And at times, tonight for example, he was wondering if such detailed knowledge was really worth the trouble. For, to tell the truth, he felt rather sick of himself.

There was, however, some excuse an impartial observer might have offered for this despondency on the part of Laureston Baker, for he was just then suffering from an attack of influenza, and influenza has an uncanny way of pricking the bubble of one's self-esteem. And to an egoist like Laureston Baker, whose bubble was of reasonably large proportions, the pricking process usually was a shattering one. How he dreaded these annual attacks of the malady! Proud of his self-sufficiency, he always loathed the realisation that on such occasions he was wholly dependent on the good graces of others: the doctor, the people at the office, the cook, the housekeeper; particularly the housekeeper, a docile and well-meaning fuss-body who, in her eager anxiety to please, caused him acute annoyance. But she was honest, though ignorant, and when he heard of what wages other people paid their servants, he could well afford to smile.

Here I am, he thought, a helpless thing in a bed. A rundown machine. I, the real I, am altogether of no consequence. I could just as well be . . . a cough shook him through and through . . . There you are, my body, this body of mine is now more than me. It coughs, it expectorates. It has me by my own throat. *I* can do nothing. Damn it.

He coughed and spat again and wiped his unshaven lips.

'Calling, sir?'

The damned old fool, he thought. Hovering around, waiting like a sick-nurse on me. Why the hell does she have to ask such silly questions? Can't she tell a cough from a call?

But he answered: 'No. No, thank you, Robinson.' For despite his inherent selfishness, he always made it a point to be most considerate to the feelings of others. He liked everybody to think well of him, and it afforded him great complacency to know that as far as Robinson was concerned, he was the kindest and most thoughtful master that could be wished for.

'Yo' wishes yo' milk now, sir?'

'Yes. Yes,' he growled.

There you are, he went on thinking, I simply can't be really sincere towards anyone. I can only pretend to be in order to gain my own ends. She'd be heartbroken, I suppose, if anything happened to me, but if she were to die tonight, I shouldn't turn a hair. Except perhaps to wonder if I could get someone who wasn't quite such a damned fool.

The bedroom door opened and Robinson entered with the milk on a tray which she placed on the table at his bedside.

'Yo' wants anything mo' tonight, sir?'

He shook his head. He'd begun coughing again.

'Best be ca'ful if yo' gets up to go to de doubleyou in de night. It still rainin'.'

God, must she stand there and watch me while I cough and expectorate, he thought. How I wish I could tell her to . . . But:

'It's all right, Robinson,' was what he said. 'I think you'd better go to bed now.'

'Yes, sir. Goodnight, sir.'

She went out, shutting the door after her. He could hear her open the back door, close it and go down the steps to the outhouse which by courtesy was referred to as her quarters.

Yes, he went on, continuing his train of thought, I can't be really sincere towards anyone. I can't think of people as existing outside their relationship towards me. Me, me, all the time. If I could only forget myself! If I could only give up my everlasting preoccupation with myself! But how is it to be done? Religion? Bunk. The very thought made him cough again. Now if I'd lived in the Middle Ages . . . But he purposely switched off the rather grandiose spectacle of himself as a scarlet-robed dignitary of the church, entering, at the head of a colourful procession, a dim-lighted Gothic cathedral with organ music in the background.

Whew . . . a slight temperature always had this effect on him.

He leaned over, jerked an aspirin out of its squat bottle and gulped it down with a sip of milk. Ugh! Nasty stuff. And Robinson would always order pints of it when he was ill. God, his throat was sore. How his head buzzed!

No. Let me get back to the point. Most certainly not religion. Not all that praying and hymn-singing. Besides, the thought of God always made him feel so insignificant. More so than astronomy even.

Love? Too old for that now. Besides, it was a greatly overrated procedure. He'd been in love twice anyhow, and he knew what he was talking about. First, with Emma, his wife. Then with Janet. And where had those experiences led? Take Emma. After two years of marriage his love for Emma had completely fizzled out, or rather fizzled into her sister, Janet. Thank God, it had fizzled out from Janet too before Emma died, else he might have got married again. And look at Janet now! A mother of five, a puncheon of humanity! And her husband, a mere breadwinner, a runner of errands, a nonentity. And where did this love, this love one reads about, lead to? When he'd been in love he'd really felt more in love with himself than with the woman. Otherwise why did he fall out of love when she'd ceased to please him? No, certainly not love.

Art? All this nonsense about what, as far as he could see, was a mere pose. He dismissed the idea from his mind. It wasn't worth consideration.

Devotion to an ideal? How the hell could anyone be devoted to the *ideal* of accountancy, he'd like to know.

How did one forget oneself in something greater?

Of course, there was always drink. It seemed to work in so many cases. But the trouble was, it always made him so horribly sick before he got anywhere. As far as he was concerned, drink was decidedly not for him.

The cough shook him again, racked him. How could one forget oneself? How could one with this constant reminder of the body's weakness, its humiliating demands? Ten to one Robinson would compel him to drink a dose of salts in the morning. Pah! What's the use of living anyway? What did he have to live for? Nothing. Nobody even to mourn him. Nobody. Nobody at all. Perhaps Robinson; yes. And Cartwright and young Steele at the office. But only for a day or two at the most. Perhaps it might be the best thing after all. He tried to think for a moment of the idea of personal extinction. But it wouldn't work. He pictured himself as a rather futile ghost hanging around corners, trying to find out what people were saying about him. But I don't want, he almost shouted aloud, to think about . . . a mighty sneeze absorbed all his corporeal faculties for a moment . . . myself.

It was then that he first became aware of the sound. It was a plaintive far-off sound, a sound which at first he could not distinguish. He listened carefully. The shutters of the window were open but the sash had been pulled down, and he could see the raindrops trickling slowly down the panes. Whatever the sound was, it was coming from out there in the darkness. It was a plaintive little sound, faint and dolorous. Whatever could it be? He could hear the monotonous drip of the water from the eaves and the mellow gurgle of the nightly chorus of whistling frogs. Then suddenly the sound was repeated, louder and more plaintive; he recognised it now. It was a kitten, a kitten mewing piteously.

The sound recalled to his mind a kitten he'd had when he was a little boy. He could see it now, a little fluffy ball of yellow-brown fur on which he had lavished all his childhood affection. Emily (he remembered he'd called her Emily because she looked like the mulatto washerwoman who called for the clothes on Mondays) had been the joy of his heart. And then, one morning she hadn't responded to his call to play. She'd sat hunched and dejected, and refused to notice him. 'Leave her alone, Laurie. She's not well. Leave her alone. She'll be all right tomorrow.' But his mother hadn't been right. Next day Emily was worse. All her beautiful silky fur was bedraggled and matted, her eyes and nose exuded mucus which had clotted loathsomely on her peaked little face. He had wanted to help her, to do something. But his mother wouldn't hear of it. Emily had been removed to the servants' closet and he hadn't seen her again till a few days later when the garden-boy had taken her pitiful corpse in a shovel to a remote corner of the garden for burial. And the next week he'd found a bit of her fur on the lawn. The dogs had dug her up and eaten her.

There was the sound again. Poor little beast, he thought. If only it wasn't raining. If only he didn't have this blasted influenza.

He gazed at the glass window more intently and suddenly he saw the kitten, crouched against the blurred pane. Its tiny nose was pressed against the glass and its questioning eyes were round and bright; and, while he watched, a raindrop spat into one of them. It blinked and mewed again.

'Robinson! Robinson!'

But of course she'd gone.

But he couldn't let the kitten look at him like that and not do something. If only it wasn't raining.

He rose to a sitting posture in the bed. Strange; he felt quite well all of a sudden. He placed the back of his hand upon his forehead. Cool as a cucumber! Now, who used to say that? Was it his wife, or his mother? Funny how things got mixed. But he certainly felt much better. The collar of his pyjamas was clammy. Fever broken and gone. Yes, he felt quite well. He tried to summon up a cough, but nothing materialised. He pushed his feet into his slippers and stood up tentatively. By all previous experience he should feel a bit giddy. But he didn't feel giddy; not the least bit. Indeed he felt so remarkably well that he could have done a jig upon the rug there and then.

'Puss, puss!' he called. 'You're coming inside, my dear!'

He crossed over to the window. And he realised gleefully that the rain had stopped. Good. He calculated how the job had best be done. First, throw up the sash window; secondly, yank puss in;

thirdly, pull down the sash window. Simple as that. By numbers. One, two, three. Elated with himself he practised the motions. Wouldn't old Robinson be surprised when she came in in the morning to find him quite well; and a newcomer in the room!

He paused. Robinson didn't like cats. She hated them. She said they gave you the tizzick. Tizzick! But what an expressive word. Gave you the tizzick and sucked your breath. Silly old fool. She'd jolly well have to run a chance of contracting the tizzick, whatever it was.

But time was passing.

One. Up went the sash.

Two. But he didn't have to pull puss in. She leapt softly into the room.

Three. But the window stuck. He pulled it but it wouldn't come down. Damn. And to make matters worse, a gust of wind sprang up and he felt the rain, cold as ice-water, beat into his face. Blast. He pulled again, and, thank goodness, it came down with a bang.

The kitten, her fur dripping wet, arched her back and made an endearing rush at his slippered feet. He bent down and picked her up. He got a towel and gave her a thorough rubbing-down. She was vibrating like a regular little engine, he thought. Then he poured out a saucerful of milk for her. She lapped it up and without even waiting to wash her face, she sprang up into the bed on which he was now sitting.

He took her up in his arms and stroked her.

'Little puss, little puss!'

Her eyes, no longer staring with anxiety and fear, were glazed over with contentment and gratitude. A wave of emotion welled up in him suddenly and he felt his eyes go damp with tears.

'Darling puss!'

Her fur had begun to dry out nicely now. How very small and helpless she was! How lovely to touch! She purred and purred. As though she, too, experienced a great happiness, her purring swelled in a crescendo that almost seemed to choke her.

Then suddenly he felt a chill seize him. Oh dear, he thought, this means I still have the 'flu. But somehow he didn't feel in the least bit worried. 'Br-r-r-r,' his teeth chattered. 'We're purring together, puss,' he gabbled, and he lay back in bed, pulling the blanket cosily about him. The kitten had got somewhat involved in this proceeding, so he released her and placed her on his stomach. But she wasn't altogether pleased to be so far away, and she climbed down the decline and nestled close to his face. Her purring was ecstatic. Outside the rain was pelting down.

'Lucky little you,' he said.

She purred harder than ever in reply.

A strange feeling of complete and utter happiness flooded him. Had he been a religious man he would probably have said, 'Thank God.' But he didn't. He thought of that other poor kitten of his boyhood. He felt at the moment that that ravaged little body, this kitten purring next to him now, he himself were all part of something in which they as individuals didn't matter very much, really. Life, death, the whistling frogs, the drip of the rain . . .

Next morning when Robinson knocked at the door, there was no answer. She knocked again. She never could hear very well, but she got the impression he was saying something which she couldn't make out at all, at all. She opened the door and went in. He was lying flat on his back and his mouth was open and he was making deep, gasping noises. She shook him. His eyes opened but there was no light of recognition in them. And then, horror-stricken, she saw curled up between the sheet and the blanket, close, close to his face, the kitten. Automatically she grabbed hold of it and with a scream dashed it with all her strength upon the ground. It gave a convulsive twitch and then lay quite still. Blind with terror and grief she rushed to the telephone.

Two days later the doctor, despite all her asseverations to the contrary, wrote down the cause of death as pneumonia.

Mark Learns Another Lesson

Mark was dressing for school. Exams were on and he felt pleasantly excited. Besides, after exams there would be Christmas shopping, watching Mother make the plum-pudding, all sorts of unusual things that happened only at Christmas. But at the moment exams were of paramount importance.

He pulled on his shoes reflectively. Could he win the Junior Class prize? Could he beat Arthur Jones? Perhaps he might get words he knew for Dictation, and he might be divinely inspired to work out at least half the sums correctly. Well, he'd been praying pretty hard during the past week. Fortified by a sense of well-doing he buttoned up his trousers and buckled his belt. If only the Dictation were reasonably easy . . .

A voice called from the outer world: 'Are you ready yet, Mark?'

'Coming now, Mother.' And off he ran.

Mother sat and watched him as he ate, chiefly to prevent him from gobbling. He was always just a little late somehow. One could play such thrilling games in the bath – there was that new one, bouncing the rubber ball against the wall amid all the spray and flurry of the shower. He glanced at the clock on the wall. Ten minutes more!

'Don't look at the clock, dear; that'll make you hurry more.'

He concentrated on the job before him. Bacon and eggs. H'm!

'Go on, dear. Don't try to put the whole egg in your mouth at once. You'll make a mess of your collar. Look . . . out!'

He wished Mother would run off and do something.

'Don't forget your lunch-money.' Mother pushed it across the table with her forefinger.

Mark made an acquiescent noise as he pursued a slithering bit of bacon around the plate.

'Mark, Mark, take time!'

'Oh, all right, Mother.'

How fussy women were! He felt quite grown-up now. In a couple of weeks' time he'd be nine years old and already he'd been at school for two whole years. He had succeeded at last in cornering the bacon and after a futile attempt to cut it up, had by a stroke of luck managed to fold it into a pleated mass which he stuck into his mouth.

Mother stared horror-stricken for a moment, then got up and left the room. Mark chuckled. Yes, one shouldn't let women affect one's line of conduct. But he'd kiss her goodbye this morning instead of letting her do everything. Poor Mother. Dear Mother!

Breakfast put away, mouth and hands sprinkled and dabbed, lunch-money and tram tickets shoved into their respective pockets, Mother duly kissed, Mark was soon waving her goodbye as he trotted down the lane to catch the tram.

Not a moment too soon. The mule-tram was already in sight, its wheels cooing pleasantly as it swept round the curve, and in another few moments had pulled up beside Mark and the other two passengers who always caught the 9.15 tram.

Mark usually hoped to get a corner seat without success, but this morning he was lucky. The driver released the brake, clicked his tongue, the pair of chubby mules strained cheerfully at the traces, and in no time the tram was rolling along the well-known road to the Driscolls'.

As Mark sat happily in his corner seat watching the familiar houses speed by, he fell to wondering how many mornings he had already made this trip. Once it had been a novelty. And going to school for the first time – what an adventure that had been! He smiled as he recalled all the unnecessary fears and unwarranted anticipations of school . . .

He remembered the first day he'd gone to the Driscolls': it had been a few days before school had begun, and Mother had taken him. The school, a two-storeyed building with an overhanging railed gallery like so many others in and near the city, was right on the street. Indeed the front door and windows always had to be kept closed, for through them anyone in a passing tram could have easily looked into the schoolroom. Mother had rapped on the jalousied door with her parasol and a deep voice had called: 'Come in. Just push the door, will you?' The room they found themselves in was a large one, along three sides of which were long desks and benches made of deal. They had been newly scrubbed and emitted a friendly smell. A few old maps hung on the walls, and directly opposite the door were a small desk and chair. Behind these was a flight of stairs. On the landing, leaning over the balustrade, was the owner of the deep voice that had bidden them come in. 'Come right up, come right up.'

They crossed the room and were greeted by Miss Driscoll on the landing.

'Excuse my not coming all the way down,' she breathed in a monstrous whisper, 'but the stairs are so severe. I try not to take them more than I possibly can.'

Mark had a very hazy idea of all that followed at that first interview; for his entire attention throughout it all had been completely absorbed by his amazed contemplation of the Miss Driscoll who had met them on the landing, and of her sister. They were fascinating, fantastically so. Miss Vi Driscoll, the owner of the voice was – Mark couldn't find a word to describe her to himself. There she sat in a very large chair and yet there were parts of her protruding all around. Her face was set amid a vast expanse of wattle-like folds and chins, and when she sighed the lower part of her face was completely obscured by a tremendous upheaval of bosom. She reminded him of nothing so much as a picture he'd seen once of a captive balloon, imperfectly blown out and wabbly. 'Enor-mious,' thought Mark. Yes, that's what she was, Enormious. But he liked her. Her mouth was round and red like a capital O, and her eyes twinkled. He wasn't so sure of the other Miss Driscoll, Miss Ket. She was gaunt and thin-lipped, spoke but seldom and had a steely glitter in her eye; but she was equally fascinating, for at intervals her tongue would shoot out, quiver and then be drawn in again, as though it possessed an individuality of its own and escaped every now and then from her control. He found himself speculating when it was due for an appearance, but he never could get it right. He was rather sorry when Mother rose to go.

'Have no fear; we'll look after your boy,' boomed Miss Vi, and Miss Ket's tongue flicked a tacit assent.

Then the first day! As he pushed open the creaky swing-door that Monday morning, Mark had entered a new phase of life. His mind had to make many rapid adjustments that day. The bewildering number of new faces, boys' and girls', the fact that each of these belonged to an individual like himself; their voices, their peculiarities, the realisation that he couldn't run to Mother to ask her advice on anything, the lessons, having to sit still for such long periods of time – all these things had to be taken in, absorbed, digested. It wasn't till the end of the week that he felt at all accustomed to his new surroundings. By that time he had struck up an acquaintance with Arthur Jones; got to know the names of all the twenty-eight boys and girls; realised he had to be very circumspect in his approach to Sammy O'Neil, the head boy; been inspired with a blind devotion to Mary Browne, the head girl, and a scornful disregard for all the other silly, frilly little things in frocks; assumed a patronising air to Dudley Dixon, a gawky stammering thirteen-year-old booby; learnt to snub Pork Watson who was supposed to smell; kept a wary eye on Miss Ket who snapped at you and sometimes rapped you on the knuckles with a ruler when you couldn't get out your sums, and learnt to carry on diverting, whispered conversations with Arthur when they came up in class for Recitation or Prayers. But usually you didn't come up in class. You sat at your desk and wrote Dictation, or worked out Sums on slates, or 'refreshed your memory' revising your homework; then at intervals you went up: one at a time, to Miss Vi who 'heard the lesson'. If your answers were satisfactory, the 'portion for next time' was marked and you went back to your seat and prepared another; if they were not, then you were 'returned' (this was supposed to be 'distressing') and you had to 'get it up' some more.

On Miss Vi's desk was an old leather strap that looked as if it had been chewed by some mischievous puppy; but it was displayed more as a symbol of office than anything else; there were really only Miss Ket's ruler and nasty looks to fear.

So Mark had found school rather like a good game. He liked reading, and found learning lessons more pleasant than otherwise.

Geography was fun. You learnt names of rivers and towns and capes and so on, and looked them up on the map. Such strange names, such friendly, comical names! The Skagerrak and Kattegat. Portland Bill and the Lizard, Amsterdam and Rotterdam, and actually – almost incredibly – the Po! Grammar, red-backed and sticky, was good too in spots: making up sentences; but for the most part it was dry and incomprehensible, especially the part on mood where the words 'might, could, would or should' repeated themselves over and over again, like the chorus of some insane nursery rhyme. History and Scripture: Hengist and Horsa, Alfred the Great, Adam and Eve, Cain and Abel – but he preferred Scripture, for History had Dates and Scripture didn't; moreover Scripture was like Puss in Boots and Jack the Giant Killer, and was illustrated. But it wasn't so easy when you came to Arithmetic. No sooner had you learnt the Tables – and you could never be absolutely certain whether 8 times 9 was 54 or 72 – you had to tackle things called Weights and Measures . . .

Mark grimaced. Arithmetic was first thing this morning too. He offered up a last incoherent prayer as the tram pulled up and he stepped out. Well, the worst would soon be over. He pushed the swing-door open and walked in.

In the few minutes that remained before the bell rang – school began at half-past nine – Mark heard that Miss Vi had told them that up to the present he was leading in the Junior Class, leading Arthur by 39 marks. He made a rapid calculation. He could afford to get four – say three – sums wrong and still keep the lead. Good.

The little cracked bell rang and there was the dreaded Arithmetic paper at last. And hooray, they hadn't set one of those things with rodspolesorperches! He could hardly believe his luck.

He could hardly believe it when at ten minutes' break he found by comparing answers he'd got only one sum wrong!

He was supremely confident when he sat down to tackle the Scripture paper. It was pie. He let himself go. He even thought of putting in a few illustrations gratis. How lovely to hear the screeching noise his OO nib made as it flowed over the smooth foolscap paper! Long before time was up he had finished. But he wasn't satisfied. He went through his paper again, correcting a word that didn't look quite right here, making an addition there . . .

Iasac and his wife Rebeca had 2 sons Esau and Jacob. Esau used to go out and hunt and Jacob didnt. Jacob wanted to get his farthers blessing so one day Iasac told Esau to go and bring him some vension and he would give him his blessing and as soon as Esau left Jacob got his mother to kill a kid and cook it.

Something was missing here. Making the little wiggle he'd been taught to do. Mark inserted carefully: *I forgot to say that Iasac was blind.*

He went on reading.

Then Jacob put on Esau's clothes and covered his hands with the skin of the kid because if Iasac touched him he would feel like Esau because Esau was a hairey man. So when Jacob brought the meat to Iasac he nearly found him out because he didnt change his voice anyway he smelt him and felt him I expect he was a bit deaf too and so Jacob fooled him and Iasac gave him his blessing and he went away and saw a ladder with angles going up and down and the Lord blessed him too. Of course when Esau came home and found out Jacob had cheated him he was mad. But he couldnt do anything and old Iasac was sorry.

As he reread the story Mark was seized with a fierce resentment against Jacob. He'd always felt that way whenever he read the story. Two clear lines of foolscap remained to be written on. He wrote rapidly. There! That completed the lot. He blotted it, arranged the sheets in order, put away his pen and ruler, carried the paper up to Miss Vi who favoured him with one of her throaty chuckles, and went back to his seat to wait till the bell rang for luncheon.

At luncheon time the marks for the Arithmetic paper were given. Arthur Jones: 90, Mark: 81. Still leading, and Arthur couldn't possibly catch up with him in the Scripture paper. If only he had a little luck in Dictation! Well, the worst would soon be over. The final results would be known that afternoon. During exams, all the children sat together and Miss Vi supervised, while Miss Ket somewhere upstairs did the corrections.

Dictation wasn't too bad; there were no unusual words, and only things like siege and seize – or was it seige and sieze? Anyway . . .

All was over. They sat around talking quietly. It was very thrilling waiting to hear the results. Occasionally one of the girls would giggle and Miss Vi would emit a sepulchral Shuh!

Mark himself had gone quite clammy. He was showing Arthur his palms when suddenly he heard Miss Ket's voice from the landing calling him.

'Come here, Mark. Come upstairs.'

Miss Ket's voice sounded queer, somehow. But as he passed Miss Vi she gave him a little growl of encouragement.

He ran up quickly. Perhaps he'd done so well Miss Ket wanted to tell him personally.

But no. Something – something was wrong. He had never seen Miss Ket's tongue do such antics before. And her eyes were unusually solemn.

'Mark!'

'Yes, Miss Ket.'

'Mark, look at me.'

Mark did so.

'Aren't you ashamed, bitterly ashamed of yourself?'

Ashamed! Whatever was she talking about? Then he noticed she was holding in her hand his Scripture paper, and that she was pointing to the last sentence on the sheet, that sentence he had inserted as an afterthought.

'Aren't you bitterly ashamed?' she repeated.

Mark's eyes opened wide.

'Aren't you?'

'I . . . I . . .'

'Of course you are, unhappy child. Don't you know . . .' her tongue flicked in and out faster than he'd ever seen it . . . 'don't you know you have written something here . . .' she tapped the offending sentence with a long fingernail, 'that might send you straight to hell?'

Mark squirmed. 'N . . . no.'

'Do you understand the meaning of what you've written, child?'

Mark glanced at it sideways to make sure. Yes, it was there just as he'd written it.

'Y . . . yes.'

'I've never heard of such a thing. Why . . .' Miss Ket was almost too shocked to say the word. 'Why, it's . . . it's blasphemy!'

That didn't help Mark, however. By this time he had got over his astonishment and fright and was wondering if Miss Ket's tongue would favour him with another of those incredible triple-flicks.

Suddenly he realised she was saying something he *could* understand.

'. . . so your getting nought for this paper completely robs you of all chance of coming among the first three in the class.'

Getting nought! He could hardly believe his ears. Why, he had worked so hard, prayed so hard . . . it was unfair! Nought! And not even a third place! Oh, it was unspeakably unfair. There was only one thing he felt he could do, should do in the circumstances. He howled.

He howled and spluttered and choked and howled some more. He went on for a considerable time. Indeed Miss Ket left him crying to go downstairs for prayers and dismissal after reading the results. After a while she returned. Miss Vi came with her.

'You must stop crying now,' boomed Miss Vi. 'We can see you're really and truly sorry for what you wrote. You must be a good boy now and pray to the Lord to forgive you.'

'And perhaps you won't go to hell if you were to die tonight,' suggested Miss Ket not unkindly.

'Wup,' sobbed Mark, a hiccupy sort of a sob.

'And we've decided not to tell your parents; it would grieve them too greatly,' continued Miss Vi.

'Not now that you're truly penitent,' added Miss Ket.

Miss Vi laid a heavy, tender hand on his shoulder. 'It's time for your tram. You'd better run along now, dear.'

'Yes, indeed,' chimed in Miss Ket.

'Goodbye,' said Miss Vi.

'Bye,' flicked Miss Ket's tongue.

'Wup,' said Mark, and groping his way blindly downstairs he collected his books. Unfair . . . unfair . . . unfair . . . the refrain went on over and over in his head. He pushed open the door as he heard the tram-whistle blow. More unfair even than that business with Jacob . . .

From their chairs in the drawing room upstairs Miss Vi and Miss Ket heard the tram stop for a moment and then continue on its way.

Miss Vi glanced once again at the sheet of foolscap in her hand and reread the damning sentence:

But it wasnt fair and I dont think the Lord acted right that time.

'Poor little fellow,' she sighed heavily. 'I'm sure he's very, very sorry for what he's done.'

'He should be,' agreed Miss Ket.

'I wonder whatever made him think of such a thing!'

'Perhaps he just didn't think at all,' flicked the tongue. 'Come on, Vi, it's time for tea.'

The Story of the Tragic Circumstances Surrounding the Death of Angela Westmore

It was only this morning that I learnt that Guff and his family had left the island.

I read the brief announcement twice to make sure, and hurried to communicate the news to Phil. He paused in his shaving, closed his eyes, and murmured, 'Thank God.' And Phil isn't what one would call a religious man.

But perhaps I'd better explain. Guff had been all along one of the minor worries and complications of existence. He had married a distant relative of Phil's, and had come to believe in consequence that he was expected to call on us from time to time. He never brought his wife with him, but would sit on for hours discoursing on such topics as he considered of interest to himself and the world at large, thereby reducing us both to a state bordering on coma, which he somehow or other chose to interpret as one of rapt interest. He was, in short, the most accomplished bore. His real name was Randolph McGuffie, and his nickname had, among his long-suffering acquaintances, acquired the signification of a transitive verb, passive voice. 'We were properly guffed last night,' was a statement which never failed to evoke sympathy. Being 'guffed', if only for an hour or two, was an experience which all his victims understood only too well.

'But you must grant he did bring us a bit of news now and then,' I said.

'Like the story of Angela Westmore's death,' Phil growled. 'Yes, I know. Breakfast nearly ready?'

As I went to get ahead with the morning routine, I reflected that perhaps the story of the death of Miss Westmore *was* Guff's masterpiece.

We hadn't known Angela Westmore personally, but the news of

her death that Sunday afternoon nearly a year ago had been a shock. She had left school only a year or two previously, was a most charming and attractive girl and was regarded as a coming tennis champion.

The news of her death, brought us by the garden-boy, was therefore completely unexpected. Every now and then we'd think of her as we'd last seen her a month before in the women's singles, the picture of youthful grace and energy: realisation of the tragedy was almost impossible. The garden-boy hadn't been able to supply any details: she had got drowned at Sandy Cove; Mr Brown, the policeman who lived up the road, had told him; it had happened at half-past four that afternoon. That was all he knew.

And a short while after, a brief announcement over the rediffusion system confirmed what he had told us.

We were both puzzled. There had never been a drowning fatality at Sandy Cove as far as either of us could remember. Besides, Angela Westmore was a good swimmer. I suggested that we might drive around – it was only six or seven miles from town – in a casual sort of way, and try to pick up what information we could. But Phil objected. Snooping, he called it. So we sat on the verandah reading, and from time to time one or other of us would venture some conjecture as to how she could have met her death in that manner.

It was growing dark. Suddenly, headlights blazing, a car swept into the gap and drew up at the door.

Phil half-raised himself from his berbice chair, peered over the balustrade, and groaned.

I raised an enquiring eyebrow.

'Guff,' he grunted.

We exchanged despairing glances, and rose to greet our visitor.

'Well,' he began ponderously, as he sank into Phil's chair, 'and how are you two?'

As this question was merely his usual gambit, we neither did more than move our lips, for Guff was ready to launch out on to a recital of the various ailments his podgy frame had accommodated during the past month or so. Certain rheumatic symptoms being in evidence on this occasion, I ventured:

'I hope all this doesn't affect your having a drink, Guff?'

'What do you think, child? What do you think?' He smiled in his most roguish manner. 'The usual. The usual.'

I almost scampered off to mix the rum and gingers. Mixing a drink for Guff offered a respite, no matter how brief.

'Sorry to keep you waiting so long,' I said when I returned almost a quarter of an hour later. 'I couldn't find the opener.'

Phil flashed a glance of near-hatred at me. 'Not so good,' he remarked sipping his drink, 'I'm mixing the next one.'

But Guff, quite oblivious of our passage at arms, continued: '. . . because it may be uric acid, though, on the other hand, as you can clearly see, it may not.'

He glanced at both of us triumphantly as though he had scored a major point in debate.

'Now the wife's mother says . . .'

And it was at this point that I suddenly had a brainwave. Guff's mother-in-law lived in one of the bungalows at Sandy Cove! It was most probable that Guff might know something of the tragedy. If we had to listen to a Guffian Ulysses, it might be just as well if it should prove, if not altogether interesting, at least informative.

'By the way,' I broke in, 'has your mother-in-law told you anything about Angela Westmore's death? However did she happen to get drowned? I mean, it's all so . . . so . . .'

Guff turned his head slowly towards me. He frowned at me. He did not like being interrupted.

'But that,' he said reprovingly, 'is just what I was going to tell you.' He leaned back, sipped his drink, replaced his glass on the arm of the berbice chair, and inflated his chest, regarding us both with his most superior smile. 'Came to tell you, in fact. You see . . .' he paused again dramatically, 'I was there!'

For the moment I was almost glad that Guff *had* come to see us. Now we would know how it had happened.

'You were *there*?'

Guff nodded portentously. As though overcome by the memory of the incident which fate had called him to witness, he pulled out his handkerchief, mopped his forehead, finished his drink at a gulp, and shook his head. 'A sad thing,' he said slowly, 'a very sad thing.'

'You saw it all?' I asked.

He held up a rebuking hand. 'I will tell you everything. From the beginning.'

There was something ominous about this statement that checked my recently experienced enthusiasm. From the beginning of . . . what? Guff was quite capable of producing a biographical disquisition on the late Miss Westmore. But his next words relieved my anxiety.

'I woke at six this morning.'

Ah, it would only be an account of one day. I sat back, prepared to make the best of it.

'Yes.' He raised his glass, regarded it intently and replaced it.

'Do the needful, dear. And I think I'll have another, too,' Phil smiled at me. Just like Phil. But this time I didn't have to look for the opener. I'd missed only the details of Guff's visit to the bathroom apparently.

' . . . so I said to Bun, "Bun," I said, "what a wonderful morning! What about our going to spend the day with the old lady?" And Bun said, "You know, Bun, I was just going to ask you the same thing."'

I should explain that Guff and his wife happen to be one of those couples who call each other by the same nickname, a practice which would often tend to make his stories even more irritating.

The two Buns being at complete accord, followed a lengthy description of the preparations. The children, Bill and June, had to be washed and fed and dressed, the garden to be watered, the pigeons seen to, and the lunch basket packed. The account of the children, garden and pigeons took about six minutes in the telling (sometimes I would relieve the tedium by checking off times on my wrist watch), and that of the preparation of the lunch basket about twice as long; for Guff fancies himself as a gourmet, and no detail was spared us. Followed then in parenthesis Guff's denunciation of canned foods, during which time I took the opportunity of mixing another drink despite Phil's plaintive reminder that it was his turn.

By this time the family had arrived at 'the old lady's' and an account of her recent problems with the domestic staff was well under way.

But neither of us dared interrupt him. The last time he'd got on to the domestic servant problem, it had led him to a sweeping denunciation of the political situation and the mistaken policy of the labour government. Shading my face as well as I could from his direct gaze, I allowed my thoughts to wander as best they might. I must have been dozing off when I caught the words Angela Westmore.

'. . . "Are you sure, Bun?" I asked. "Of course, Bun, I'm quite sure," Bun said. So she came in. "May I use the telephone?" Well, you'll understand, I couldn't help hearing what she said. She was putting a call through to young Walters, the younger brother who works at Walters Brothers. You know.'

We didn't, but we knew better than to ask for information.

'"I'm waiting for you," she said. That was all. Then she put down the receiver, thanked us and went out. Now, I ask you, wasn't that very odd?'

We signified mutely that it was.

'Very odd indeed. And I believe, though I can't prove it, mind you, that there was something fishy going on.' He lowered his voice. 'People have been talking recently, you know. It's a small community . . . Remember the Gordon affair?'

We both nodded hastily. The Gordon affair was one of Guff's pet themes.

'So about half an hour later . . .' He paused. 'No. It was about twenty minutes later, we went down for a dip. Bill and June had had a bathe already of course, but we allowed them to come with us. Bun thought it might have been too much for them, but I said to Bun, "Bun," I said, "remember when you were a kid. I'll bet you had more than one sea-bathe a day!"' He paused here with a knowing chuckle, and I watched Phil's face, eyes half-closed, trying to assume some suitable expression of interest.

'I remember once . . . I was ten or eleven . . .'

This time when I went to get drinks I took the opportunity to lay the table for supper as well. Fortunately it was cook's evening off. She at least would be spared our apologies.

They had all come out of the sea when I returned, and by what devious paths I know not, Guff's story had rambled off into the byways of the ill effects of schooner travel. Phil had slumped down in his chair so that only one eye was visible. It glowered.

I had lost all interest in the circumstances surrounding the fate of Miss Westmore by this time, and my only consolation was that, it being now nearly eight o'clock, Guff would soon have to depart for his supper. So I relaxed into a sort of simmering stupor while Guff went on and on . . . now it was sea-sickness, now the old lady's turtle steaks, now something that one Bun had said to the other, or that the other Bun had said to the one, and, occasionally, some reference to Angela Westmore – her lying sun-bathing for over two hours on the beach, her shapely legs, her flirtations, her brother-in-law's sister . . .

Through the still night air I heard the fussy little cackle of the prison-bell half a mile away.

Half-past eight! Thank God, I'd managed to escape some of the torture. Where was he now?

'By this time it was nearly four o'clock, so I said to Bun, "Bun," I said, "I think we'd be better getting on." So we packed up, said goodbye and drove down.'

So I'd missed the climax of the story after all. Well, I was too exhausted, too annoyed to care. Phil could tell me later.

'Well, we drove down. The children were sleepy, and Bill can't take too much exertion after his operation. But they'd had a good time. And, would you believe it? No sooner had I parked the car in the garage, gone upstairs and settled down to read – I hadn't seen the paper yet for the day, mind you – when the telephone bell rang.'

He paused and examined his empty glass, but neither Phil nor I stirred.

He sighed. 'Well, it was the old lady. I thought it very strange she should be calling us so soon. I thought perhaps we'd left something. Bun is always forgetting to pack things back properly. I remember . . .'

But Phil's patience was exhausted. There was a nasty note in his question: 'Yes, yes, but what did she say?'

'Well may you ask what she said; for no sooner had I taken up the receiver, when I heard her say, "Guff," she said, "would you believe it? Such a dreadful thing has happened! The beach is swarming with people, everything is in an uproar . . . poor Angela Westmore is drowned!"'

'I tell you, when I heard those words, you could have knocked me over with a feather.'

He heaved himself slowly out of the depths of the chair and towered over us triumphantly. 'Yes. That was what she had to say. Angela Westmore. Drowned. I tell you, you could have knocked me over with a feather.'

'So that was how she got drowned, eh?' asked Phil just a shade too ironically, I thought.

'Yes, sir. I thought you two would like to know the details.'

We staggered to our feet. We were both speechless.

'Well, I must be toddling. Night-night.' He shook hands with us warmly, and we watched him descend the steps with the air of one who has accomplished an important and delicate mission, clamber into the car, start up, call out another cheery night-night and drive away.

We watched his departure in silence, silence tempered with something that was almost awe.

The Man Who Loved Attending Funerals

I have a strange admission to make; but, since I regard myself as already dead, I have no reason to conceal anything: these words of mine are, as far as anything written by mortal hand can be, the truth.

I am fully persuaded that among our manifold emotional interests and activities there is some one or other which, very often unacknowledged, perhaps even unsuspected, is nevertheless the ruling and abiding passion; and this passion may range from those of the crudest and most blatant forms of expression, through an infinity of subtle changes, to others, so unusual, and, at times, so inexplicable, as to evoke from us halting excuses, if not a positive denial.

I make no such excuse or denial: my great passion on earth has been the attending of funerals.

Perhaps this may not be such a strange admission after all: there is something in each and every one of us, especially as we grow older, that tends to receive a sort of satisfaction, a happy consolation, in attending the funeral of some old acquaintance: we are not so much rejoicing that the man whom we knew in his boyhood days is gone from us for ever, but that we, perhaps as the result of our own excellence, or else perhaps safeguarded by some especial providence, have been successful in continuing this business of living, and to observe yet another of our contemporaries fall out of line. This, I think, will be reluctantly admitted by all, especially by those who have their best days behind them, and who, by dint of careful and temperate living, have so far escaped the inevitable end. Each funeral attended is, as it were, a triumphant feather in our cap registering our defiance of fate; and we hold up our heads the bolder, almost convincing ourselves that we shall continue indefinitely to escape the essential condition of mortality.

And, alas, in my particular case, I *had* succeeded in thus convincing myself: until this afternoon I was assured that this matter of dying, of being for ever hidden beneath the green surface of the earth, was not for me; rather, that this procedure, which I had viewed so often, was indeed a performance enacted for my own personal benefit, from which I should always continue to derive an ever-increasing aesthetic delight.

I cannot hope to explain the sources of this delight: my understanding of the nature of the aesthetic response or of the laws of psychology are too superficial to permit me to make any attempt to do so; but of one thing I am quite sure: there was no sadistic strain in my pleasure, no suggestion of deliberate enjoyment in the grief of those left behind to mourn, no relish in the thought that the deceased had met with a final punishment. Very often, on the contrary, mingled with that sense of rapture with which funerals alone could provide me, I experienced a state of profound melancholy and loss, of sympathy with the mourners, of compassion for all suffering humanity.

It was always thus with me. Among the earliest recollections of my childhood years, there stand out boldest those of my disposing by burial of the corpses of such of our household pets or feathered stock as happened to have died from natural causes. I grieved at their deaths, but rejoiced at their inhumation. And, very often when there was no obliging little corpse to hand, I would bury one of my dolls. There was a lovely little cemetery in one corner of our garden which came into being under my devoted hands.

At the age of nine I attended my first real funeral, my father's. I can still recall every moment of that sunny, windswept afternoon.

And, as I grew older, I would pester my mother to allow me to go to the funerals of any of our relatives or friends or important persons in the community of whose deaths I might have heard. And, more often than not, she would allow me to go with one of my uncles.

And how I admired the elegant costumes of the gentlemen: the impressive, fascinating frock coats and top hats, their suave and mysterious blackness, their stateliness, their pageantry, their austerity: proud symbols of the dignity and authority of man! My mother's gift to me on my twenty-first birthday was such an outfit. But, alas, the wearing of the frock coat was a fashion whose days were already numbered. I compromised, later, with the morning coat; during the passing of the years my wardrobe has never been without two or three of these most necessary garments.

In our small community there are few opportunities for one to appear thus formally clad: an infrequent wedding, some official function, perhaps. I could, of course, have continued the old custom of attending church services, but at an early age I had become an agnostic, and therefore not even my vanity would allow me to distress my conscience thus. But there were many other far more important occasions.

You may conclude from the foregoing that my personal vanity was a prime motive for what was fast becoming my overruling passion. But I assure you that this was not so. Always a fine figure of a man, I admit that I derived no small degree of satisfaction on appearing in correct attire at all the funerals I attended: and I must confess, for I wish to conceal not even my most secret offences, that I tended to despise and regard with unmixed contempt those who dared venture into the precincts of death not properly dressed; but all this was purely coincidental, relatively unimportant.

You may think it strange in me, morbid perhaps, that such should have been my chief preoccupation, when other young men, of my own age, were playing games, dancing, drinking, wenching, falling in love, getting married, and making their homes secure for themselves and their children.

I never had any desire to participate in games of any kind: in the tropics the sun works havoc with one's complexion. I had no hobbies beyond a brief excursion in philately, rudely terminated by the dishonesty of a close friend. (And I must confess here in parenthesis that his was one of the very few funerals at which my delight was not unreservedly aesthetic.) Dancing bored me; I had no sense of rhythm. My hesitant experiments in drinking and sexual indulgence left me nauseated. I had no talent for music or for art, and appreciation of them was quite beyond me. I read quite a great deal, biography especially. Poetry I could not understand, and the novel I found distressingly vulgar. I had not the necessary mental equipment to take more than a cursory interest in the scientific discoveries of our times.

I never married. I never met a woman to whom I could accord perfection, and I was determined that nothing short of perfection would entice me to surrender my peace of mind to the exigencies of the marital state; moreover the financial complexities of such a state dismayed me. I did fall in love once, but of that I shall speak in its proper context. When my dear mother departed this life, there remained my three sisters to whom I could always, until but recently, look for companionship, affection, and consolation. I led a very happy, if uneventful life. I worked hard at the office; I earned the respect and warm regard of my employers; in time I was admitted into partnership in the business. I have never known what it is like to be ill for even a day. A careful observer, unacquainted with me, could never have imagined that I was nearly sixty years of age.

And so, for many years I pursued my methodical, completely satisfying way of living. Indeed, I became something of a local celebrity. I had even heard it said that it could not be claimed for anyone who was someone in our community to have been properly interred unless I was present. And, to my credit, I think, I must state that I allowed no social distinction to influence my attendance. Rich or poor; white or coloured: it was sufficient for me to have known the individual in question, or to be acquainted with one or other of the bereaved relatives – I say nothing, of course, of all those whom I knew personally – for me to put in an appearance. I always went alone, for I had discovered at an early age that my friends were not always as meticulous as I in their choice of attire, and I was always conscious, if I may thus express it, of the subtle frisson of admiration, I might almost say, of mental applause, that ran through the gathering on my arrival. Many other faces were almost as familiar as mine on such occasions, for I would not have you think that this passion of mine is an altogether singular one; but I can safely assert, and prove my assertion, that I had outdistanced my nearest rival by ten point five to one. For from my seventeenth year I have kept a careful compilation of these attendances. Over this period of time they average about thirteen a month. If one multiplies this figure by the necessary number of months and years (I have already mentioned that I am nearly sixty: fifty-nine and one month to be quite exact), one will have a pretty fair idea of my performance.

I do not mind admitting that in my early days, before I was in a position to purchase either a carriage or a car, this matter of transport proved a rather expensive item on my budget. But on this score I have no regrets. I was always thrifty, and, as I have stated already, even in those far off days, I had few vices. No: I always lived quietly, returning home from the office, taking my afternoon stroll, that is, when I was not engaged in my recreation, discussing with my dear sisters (all, alas, now departed: Elspeth, the last to go, died last November) the topics of the day; retiring for the night happy in the knowledge of having committed no misdemeanour, of leaving no duty undone; and awaking next morning, fresh as the proverbial daisy, and, as far as was consonant with my dignity, scampering downstairs to turn with eager expectancy to the obituary notices in the morning newspaper.

And now I must make a further admission, one of far-reaching importance and consequence. As the years went by, some time about my forty-ninth year to be more exact, I made a startling discovery: I was able to foretell the approach of death from a close observation of the faces of those whom I would meet from time to time at funeral gatherings. I cannot hope to explain *how* I knew; all I can say is that it was quite some time before I was consciously aware of this rare gift that had been bestowed upon me; but indeed, I almost refused to credit it, until, as the result of a series of tests, most rigorously conducted, I was under no possible doubt whatsoever. I would note someone or other at a funeral, would perceive some unaccountable and unwonted something in his expression, some unmistakable token, the significance of which could point to but one conclusion. It was indeed as though I had acquired the power of glimpsing, for one fleeting and rewarding moment, the hollow energy of the underlying skull peering through its mask of dissolving flesh. And I would find myself saying to myself, in as matter of fact a way as one might similarly congratulate oneself on being alive on such and such a beautiful day, 'Well, old man, it won't be long for *you* now,' and in a comparatively short while I would find myself reading his obituary notice.

I began to scrutinise the faces of persons more closely, to make more elaborate computations; and I discovered that it became increasingly more simple for me to foretell the death of the person under observation. In fact, during this last year I was seldom off more than a day or two at most.

You will therefore understand that this perusal of the obituary notices in the morning newspapers had become more than a mere matter of information: they contained the confirmation of my judgement; and I see no reason to disguise the fact that this afforded me considerable pride.

I must withdraw the reservation stated at the end of the fourth preceding paragraph: I would literally scamper downstairs.

So it came about that this morning on making my descent I slipped and struck my head against the balustrade. I was stunned for a moment. It left me an ugly bruise on my forehead, and I was annoyed with myself. Such a thing had never happened to me before. And to increase my discomfiture, on turning to the important page in the paper, I read that Mary Ellen Wye was to be buried that afternoon. I was indeed exceedingly hurt that one or other of her brothers had not notified me personally. True, I had not seen the deceased lady for well over twenty years, had not conversed with her for nearly twice as long a time; yet I saw her brothers very often, and, to a certain extent, I still regarded myself as one of the family. For I must tell you that many years ago Mary Ellen and I had almost become engaged to be married. Of all the young women I had ever known, she, and she alone, most closely approached that quality of perfection of which I have spoken. Almost, but not quite attained it, for, despite the fact that we had all grown up together, it was not until I had broached the subject of our impending engagement to my mother and sisters that I learnt with amazement and horror that her grandmother had been the illegitimate child of a garrison officer and a common servant-girl.

She had never married. And now she was dead. Somehow the knowledge that I would be going to her funeral depressed me.

This state of depression was a novel experience. It was quite beyond my comprehension.

I went to the office, as usual; I sent a wreath to her home; but I could feel none of that excitement, none of the usual emotions, which such a treat in store usually engendered, flood my being.

I came home early. I was irritated by the unsightly bruise on my forehead. It was very painful to the touch, and I realised it would be quite impossible for me to don my top hat. Very well, I would go (I almost smiled to myself as I realised how I was being forced into doing what I had so long inveighed against) bare-headed. I had a cup of tea. I began to dress.

Then I had a sudden spell of dizziness. I had to recline on my bed for some time before I could complete my toilet. I looked at my watch. It was already eleven minutes past five. I should have to hurry.

It was a bright afternoon. A bank of sullen cloud hung low in the west; there was but little breeze; an unusual coppery glow seemed to pervade everything.

The funeral was, fortunately, at St Moystyn's on the outskirts of the city, only half a mile away. There is little or no traffic at this time of evening, and I was soon there. I parked my car and glanced anxiously at my watch. But, as I entered the quaint little churchyard, I realised how very late I was: the coffin had already been borne to the family vault. The parson was more than halfway through the service. I stood still for a moment, looking at the gathering, and I experienced a sensation of profound disgust. God, I thought, what is our society coming to! Among them all, except for the undertaker in his ill-fitting tubular costume of shiny black, there wasn't another single soul, except one of Mary Ellen's brothers, who wasn't in ordinary everyday wear: tweeds, serges, gaberdines of various shades of blue, grey and brown: a sorry sight to contemplate. They might have been a group of nondescripts chosen haphazardly from a cocktail party. My annoyance and depression were intensified by this shocking spectacle. I shuddered, and involuntarily drawing myself up to my full height, I joined them.

I have already mentioned the strange coppery glow of the evening; in this garish light everything appeared slightly different somehow. And as I blinked my eyes and looked around me, I could hardly give credence to what I saw. At first I thought it might have been some trickery of the weird light, but after a moment's consideration I was positive that it was not; for, as I glanced from one face to another, I became aware, completely and without any shadow of doubt, that the dread impress of imminent dissolution, of which I have already spoken, lay stark upon almost each and every one of those present. It was altogether astonishing, and, needless to say, quite unprecedented. There was standing next to me John Wadell, the accountant. His skin was the colour of that of a man stricken with acute jaundice; the flesh hung in flaccid wattles from his face, his eyes were completely empty of expression or purpose. Indeed, as far as I was concerned, he might have been already dead, as he stood there, his eyes staring into nothingness. Beside him was Dr Hope, for years my sisters' medical practitioner. A ruddy-faced old fellow, he now looked bleached; such colour as remained in his baggy cheeks might have been daubed on by some inexperienced hand at an amateur theatrical performance: you could almost see the blood being slowly drained out of him to coagulate in those two unhealthy splotches. And as I hastily glanced from one face to another near by, at the face of Manley Davis, the dry goods merchant, at that of Arthur Grimswold of Grimswold Mansions, even at those of the comparatively young King-Lord twins, born on my thirtieth birthday, I could see only leaden faces, saffron faces, waxen faces, livid faces, all of them almost drained of their living essence, all sealed with the sure expectancy of swiftly approaching death.

And as I stood there, speculating on the nature of the oncoming epidemic which was to dispense such wholesale mortality, the full import of what I had seen almost overwhelmed me. Gone were the petty annoyances and depressions of the day; I was caught up in something so stupendous that I could only with difficulty conceal my excitement. I felt myself possessed with a sense of more than physical exhilaration; almost as though, and I hope you will understand what I am trying to express, for I can find no other way of describing it, almost as though I were in process of becoming a god. I state this in all truthfulness, and, I venture to say, in all humility. But this is how it appeared to me. Here I was, aware of all these petty mortals, clustered in ant-like formation about the grave, aware of their absurd limitation, and so far, far above them in the plenitude of my omniscience. I regarded them with a sense of overweening contempt and scorn; yet, in some strange way, there was in my exalted state of soaring ecstasy, still room for pity.

I note this extenuating circumstance at this moment with some small degree of satisfaction. God knows, I, too, am in dire need of pity, now.

The vault sealed, the wreaths laid on, the mourners moved away in bleak groups. I advanced and shook hands, murmuring a few conventional words of sympathy with the brothers who all, I was surprised to observe, despite the imprint of death on their faces, regarded me somewhat strangely: there was in their attitude not only an ill-disguised disapproval of seeing me there, but almost, though I could not understand it at the time, a recoiling such as might have been due to some physical revulsion. Perhaps it was the bruise on my forehead, I thought, for it was, I am compelled to admit, an ugly sight: or was it that I was without my top hat? For I could not, would not, believe that they grudged my paying my last respects to the woman whom they had said often enough I had callously jilted.

But even this ungraciousness on their part could not adversely affect my demeanour towards them. I shook hands with them compassionately, not only on account of their bereavement, but forgiving them their resentment, everything, in the certain knowledge that within three months at most, all three of them, Willy the eminent solicitor, Herbert the MCP, and Arthur, poor shiftless Arthur who had never done an honest day's work in all his life, would be occupying, well, if not the vault with Mary Ellen, some other, or else some cubic feet of space beneath the mould. It was so sad that I could almost have afforded to impart to my words of sympathy a sincerity which I do not often experience. But, infused as I was with this secret knowledge and sense of superhuman power, it was all I could do to prevent myself from shrieking with laughter. Yes, Herbert, the dignified Herbert, one of the few remaining adherents to correct attire for every occasion, would be the first to go. It would be less than a fortnight for him.

The light filtered through the spreading, bare limbs of the flamboyants, gathering, as the evening progressed, more and more intensity; the corpse faces passed me by and departed. I watched them all go. And then I could give way to my laughter, for I knew that for most of them, the next time they attended a funeral ceremony it would be they who would play the all-important role.

The uncanny light flooded the sky. I looked up to it and stretched out arms to it: almost a sacramental gesture, a symbol, as it were, of my apotheosis.

After a few moments I walked out of the churchyard and approached my car. Never have I felt so completely and absolutely at one with everyone and everything. I could have danced my way home. As I drew near the car, I noticed that two little urchins were peeping into it, fingering something. I shouted at them, and they jumped down and ran away.

I got into the car, noticing without surprise that my forehead was aching, had been aching, indeed, all the time. But this was of no consequence. I remember I began to sing. And then I observed that something was wrong. Those two urchins had been fiddling with my rear-view mirror. It was facing the setting sun and the unearthly light appeared to be focused directly upon it. I leaned forward to adjust it.

And, as I did so, I saw, peering into it, a face, such a face as I have never seen, a face which I am determined never to see again. For it was the face of death itself: the remorseless blank eyes, void of every hope or fear known to mortal men, staring from a torn covering of all but putrescent flesh; and, as in an X-ray photograph, through the shadowy open mouth, arrested in an attitude of song, the vacuous grin of the abiding skeleton.

I looked around. Who in God's name, could be playing such a ghastly joke on me? It was quite a little while before I realised I was gazing at my own reflection in the rear-view mirror of my car.

It is now eight minutes past midnight. I have finished with exactly twelve minutes to spare. I have already written Herbert Wye asking him to make all the necessary arrangements. Whom else can I ask? There must be at least one person there suitably attired.

Rewards and Chrysanthemums

The chrysanthemums formed a solid yellow square in the far corner of the garden. They were the first thing Joan saw every morning when, before dressing, she limped across the room to draw the curtains. Usually the garden-boy would be watering them, but this morning he was not there. But then it was the day before Christmas; he'd probably turn up later, full of excuses. No one she'd ever encountered had a more ready supply of excuses than that garden-boy.

Joan paused before drawing the curtains. It was yet too early for the customary early morning procession of children and nurses, businessmen in shining cars, and hucksters with trays of greens.

The garden was not more than ten or twelve yards wide, and the yellow chrysanthemums were separated from the street only by a low wire fence. Across the way there was an open raw spot of land. Aberystwyth Gardens was still in process of construction and Joan was glad that thus far there was no bungalow there. She could look past the empty lot, over the open fields of sour-grass to the background of low hills, their flanks scarred with quarries. No doubt some of their stone blocks would soon be scattered right before her bedroom window amidst a babble of masons and carpenters; but she hoped the day would be far off. Maud, her sister and benefactress, held altogether different views. 'You never had any sense of tidiness or propriety, Joan. You can't tell how that sore patch irritates me. I hope the Wellworths decide to buy. If they build there I'm sure it'll be a credit to the neighbourhood.'

Maud's chrysanthemums had been. Almost everyone stopped to admire them.

Joan focused her attention upon them once again. There was something about them that was distasteful, sinister almost. Try as she might, she could not account for her involuntary dislike of them. She was sure it was not their effusive yellowness, nor was it their stiff regimentation. Whatever it was, she would not let it worry her. She drew the curtains and began to dress.

But, as she hobbled about the room, she found that she could not thus easily dismiss the question from her mind. Why did the sight of those chrysanthemums every morning as she woke depress her, fill her with foreboding?

She was growing old, that's what it was, old, and full of morbid fancies. Only yesterday Maud had told her 'You're not a young woman, Joan, but there's no reason why you should mope about the house. I'm well aware that you can't do much now,' with a glance at her injured foot, 'but at least you might be thankful you've a roof over your head, something to eat every day, and a sister to look after you. Why don't you take up a book and read?'

But then this was the sort of thing Maud would tell her almost every day, and what made it worse was that she had no reply. For despite Maud's complete lack of graciousness, she had most certainly acted the part of the kind, forgiving sister. No, she could not blame Maud. Maud had led an altogether respectable life. Born some sixty years ago in the parish of St Mary, of parents who had partly succeeded in emerging from the status of 'poor-whites', she had, when the family finally came to town, met and married at the right time the right man (salt fish and pickled snouts) and, just at the right time, he had died, leaving her quite well off. There had been no children. Solid investments ensured her an income which enabled her to live in respectable comfort, with a cook, a maid and a garden-boy; and the garden, bridge parties, novels designated as 'romances', and frequent orgies of church-going provided her spiritual needs. It was all the more to Maud's credit that despite this background of eminent respectability she should have invited her erring younger sister whom she had neither seen nor heard of for over twenty years, and whose life, judged even by the most tolerant, must have been regarded as unconventional to say the least, to return to Barbados and share her home and all its comforts.

Sitting on the elegant low stool and brushing her greying hair slowly, Joan contemplated her reflection in the elaborate mirror.

At forty-eight, she found it increasingly difficult to believe she had been once considered beautiful; those last few years, the degradation of that loathsome apartment house, that frightful accident, had played their contributory parts too well. She was lucky, as Maud was never tired of reminding her, to have survived it all. She fingered the long scar that stretched across her right cheek, and the toes of her crippled foot twitched in involuntary sympathy. It was indeed difficult to believe that up to not so very long ago men had found her desirable; that she had, as Maud had solemnly though not too indelicately reminded her, lived with several of them (but then Maud always liked to exaggerate: there had been only three); and that for five unforgettable years she had found a happiness which, despite its tragic conclusion, she was ever thankful to have experienced.

She had once tried to tell Maud the story of that redeeming interlude, but her sister, shocked and outraged, had refused to listen. She did not try again.

Joan sighed resignedly. She had long since made up her mind that no matter how hurtful her sister's remarks might be, no matter how impervious her mind to everything beyond its circumscribed range of conventionality, she would never, no matter how great the provocation, do anything but accept all this as part of life's many tribulations; for she knew this proceeded not from any desire to wound but from self-righteousness and a complete lack of sensibility. Of her inherent kindness and sincere affection she had no doubt whatever.

Voices from the garden attracted her attention: those of Maud and the garden-boy. Maud was giving instructions about the chrysanthemums. Those wretched chrysanthemums again.

Joan hobbled over to the window.

Maud was standing, sheaves of the golden flowers in her arms, and the garden-boy was attacking the plot furiously, his teeth flashing in a wicked grin as though he was only too glad to be revenged upon the flowers that had taken up so much of his time during the past few weeks.

'Churchill, Churchill, don't be so violent, I tell you!'

But Churchill's only reaction to these words was a wider grin, and Maud, laying the cut chrysanthemums on the grass, approached him menacingly.

Joan turned from the window with a smile. These passages at arms were almost of daily occurrence. However Maud managed to put up with the little rascal was more than Joan could understand. Maud's explanation was simple: 'That boy came to me in peculiar circumstances, my dear. He walked in here one morning and told me he had a dream, and that in the dream the Lord had told him to come and apply for a job at the lady in the new house. I mean, can you imagine a boy like that making up such a story? No. I'm convinced the Lord really did send him to me, and I'm going to see to it that He didn't send him in vain. I'm going to make something out of him all right. Besides, with a name like that, he should go far.'

And in an even more roundabout though no less authenticated manner, Maud was convinced of the Lord's hand in leading her erring sister back to her receptive bosom. Maud was never tired of relating the circumstances to all her friends and relations; and, though at first Joan had found the story profoundly embarrassing, she had learnt to realise that its repeated recitation had become almost a justification of its narrator's existence. 'Yes, a stranger, a perfect stranger, child. I met him at the Walter Joneses'. Suppose I hadn't gone there to bridge that afternoon! And I'd had such neuralgia all day. Well, we were talking of this, that and t'other, and he told me of this poor woman who'd been in a street accident in Brooklyn . . . of course the reason he mentioned it was because he was a visiting surgeon at this hospital, and there it was written on her card: "Place of birth: Barbados", and he wondered if we, Barbadians . . . you see, he'd only arrived in the island that very day and you know how the Walter Joneses get hold of all these *new* people, they just have to be introduced to a foreigner and they ask him to their home . . . and, well, he wondered if any of us happened to know of any Barbadian family by that name, and well, just fancy, my sister, my own sister.'

At first Joan had reminded her that it was fortunate she'd never got married, else the name wouldn't have meant anything, but Maud had reproved her severely: 'You were always a scoffer, Joan. Besides, if you had got married and led a proper life, you wouldn't have had to work for a living and live in that wretched apartment place in the Brooklyn slums, and you wouldn't . . .'

So Joan had never interrupted her again. And Maud would continue at great length and attention to detail how the doctor had on his return traced the whereabouts of her sister, and how, thanks to his kind offices, all arrangements had been made for her return, and of all the bother with officials and steamship agents, and . . . well, there she was and little the worse for the accident except for the injured foot. And the scar, of course.

Yes, Churchill and herself had much to be thankful for, Joan mused: the reformatory at best for him, and for her . . . She shuddered at the memory of the sordid room she had occupied during those last months, and of the gas stove, filthy with the grease of years, the way to finality.

It wasn't until she peeped into Maud's shining kitchen where the kettle was humming cosily on the counterpart of that other nightmare that she was able to shake off her mood of depression. Maud was sticking the chrysanthemums into a couple of large vases. She turned and greeted Joan breathlessly.

'There now, there you are! Aren't they lovely?'

Blinking rapidly behind the elaborately contrived spectacles, Maud's eyes, usually pale yellow, seemed almost golden in the reflected light from the flowers. Like them, she sparkled, and her pudgy frame, bulging in all the expected places, quivered with delight.

'Aren't they beau-tiful?' She fingered the blooms lovingly.

And then her whole personality seemed to wilt, the gleam faded from her eyes: 'Ah-h-h, who knows when someone will be doing this for us?'

This abrupt change of mood in Maud was something that Joan had long since grown accustomed to, though she could never quite comprehend the process by means of which these startling transitions were effected; but on this occasion the cause of the change and the question that accompanied it were unusually mysterious.

'Doing what, Maud?'

Maud regarded her pityingly. 'Really, I think there are times when you just mean to irritate me.' She wiped her hands on the extra-large kitchen-towel hanging from the rack beside her, and, taking the kettle off the stove, set about getting the morning coffee ready.

'But . . . I don't understand . . .'

'Of course it's America that's done all this to you; and besides, you never had any sense of what is right and proper. Fancy your forgetting! Don't you know what today is?'

'It's Christmas Eve.'

'Exactly. And yet you say you don't understand. Won't, you mean.'

Joan scratched, bewildered, among her early memories: Christmas Eve . . . chrysanthemums . . . yes, it was there, somewhere among the childhood litter, that vague repulsion . . . and a pair of tight shoes. What had shoes to do with it?

'Remember?'

Wait. Wait. Something after all. Only a flickering picture: I hate them. I hate them. And the long walk down the winding hill to the parish church. And the shoes that pinched. And herself sobbing, sobbing at the injustice of it all.

'Ah, I see you do. Come and get your coffee.'

Down the winding hill. And the little barefooted urchins at the corner mocking her, pretending to cry too. Into the moss-green churchyard. Holding a huge bunch of the yellow things.

'Why, everybody takes chrysanthemums on Christmas Eve to the graves of their loved ones.'

Of course. There it all was now. The families placing their memorial bunches on the graves. And her mother prodding her from behind with her parasol. And her placing them after all, none too reverently, beneath the crooked tombstone, and the long, long walk up the hill afterwards, and those horrid shoes, and the terrific rumpus at home when Papa was told of her conduct, and all the fun of Christmas spoilt, irretrievably spoilt . . .

'Yes, I remember. And you still do?'

'Naturally. Every year these hands have laid them on our family grave. Come, child, don't stand there dreaming.' And, as she poured out the coffee, she beamed again. 'You know what, my dear? I've ordered a car to take us to St Mary's this afternoon.'

She held up a hand as Joan was about to reply. 'It'll be your first visit to the parish for ages and you'll be able to see all the old scenes again. I know you've been longing to. Only the old home isn't there any longer, of course. But never mind: I've such a nice surprise in store for you. A sort of Christmas present.'

Joan, taking her seat at the little table, leaned forward and pressed her sister's hand. Never before had she come so near understanding that undiluted, almost ridiculous blend of sentimentality and thoughtfulness that was her sister's priceless possession.

'That's very sweet of you, Maud.'

'Come, come, child, don't thank me. Look at the time! And we haven't even had our coffee yet.'

Christmas Eve was always a very busy day for Maud: so many last-minute things to be attended to, so many orders to be given her domestic staff, so many telephone calls to be put through; but throughout it all Joan could not help observing that her sister would frequently glance at her with a smile, a secret, portentous smile, which she found a little disturbing.

But the only answer Maud would give when questioned was: 'It's a Christmas present. Won't be a surprise if I tell you.'

The hired car – Maud refused to call it a taxi – was a bit late, and it wasn't until nearly five o'clock that Joan found herself gazing at the cherished landmarks as they sped along the winding country road to St Mary's: the rustling fields of wind-tossed sugar cane, their arrows rosy in the afternoon sunlight, the rounded green hills that suddenly appeared at the turning where Papa's horse had once stumbled and fallen, the old silk-cotton tree leaning across the road-way, the jumble of huts nestling among the banana and the breadfruit trees, the entrance to the deep green gully, the plantation house – how in those early days they had envied its occupants and listened some nights to the revelry that went on there! – the windmill, only an empty carcass now – all so well-remembered, so linked with those girlhood days. She squeezed Maud's hand appreciatively. If this was the surprise, it couldn't have been better planned.

Only, at the bend of the hill, where once their old home had stood, a brand new service station flashed by in a glare of red and yellow.

'It was all falling to pieces, you know. We got a good price for the land,' Maud reminded her.

But the happy memories were effaced: only a sense of the remorselessness of time's flight remained, and this mood persisted as they drove down the hill to the church. Not even the childhood illusion that all the houses were built askew along the swift slope, an illusion that recurred as the car shuddered down in low gear, could dispel her fit of depression.

The chauffeur negotiated the taxi safely around the sharp entrance to the churchyard and drew up under the moss-stained walls of St Mary's.

As they got out Joan scarcely glanced around. It was as though she had been coming to church there all through the years. Nothing seemed changed. The place had always frightened her a little. She grasped one of the bunches of chrysanthemums that Maud handed her and hobbled after her.

The sun was hanging low behind the dark frieze of the mahoganies; the frangipanis writhed along the low wall. A green dampness pervaded everything. A blue mist was creeping up behind the hill from the sea. A few old ladies and one tall gentleman in black were the only other occupants of the churchyard, and they were now, with apprehensive glances skyward, taking their departure; clusters of freshly picked flowers, chrysanthemums chiefly, lying on the scattered grass-grown mounds testified to their already accomplished mission.

Joan shivered.

Maud moved forward briskly; framed within its circumambience of chrysanthemums, her face shone with excited delight. 'Hurry, hurry,' she puffed. 'Rain.'

Joan limped after her dejectedly.

The ceremony was soon completed. Maud arranged all the flowers tastefully, prodding them into suitable positions swiftly and carefully, and then stepped back to admire the effect.

'There now, aren't they lovely? I wonder who'll be doing this for us one day. There's only Phillip's children left and they're all in Trinidad . . .' A few drops of rain pattered down and roused her from reverie.

'Oh dear, oh dear, the rain's down. But we must, we must . . .'

She grabbed Joan's arm and tugged her along. 'Come quick, quick. We must, we must. Your Christmas present.'

Completely ignoring the increasing volume of the shower, she continued to drag her sister across the slippery pathway to the other end of the churchyard where a neat square of trimly mown grass lay enclosed by an elegant wrought-iron fence.

Maud halted before it and pointed to it proudly. 'There!' she announced.

'But what . . . what . . . whose . . . ?'

Maud placed her arm around Joan and squeezed her affectionately. Her face was alight with sisterly devotion, and her eyes, behind the spectacles dimmed with raindrops, brimmed over with more than joy.

'It's for *us*, dear, it's for you and I when we pass on.' She paused to sneeze. 'There now, my darling, aren't you delighted?'

RSVP to Mrs Bush-Hall

It was to be the most wonderful party ever. Something that would be talked about for many a long day, something that would take up at least a column in *Carib*, something that would make her, Maude Bush-Hall, the most envied of mothers in Barbados. For at the party there would be the announcement of her daughter's engagement – not to a mere civil service clerk, not even to one of the local big shots, but, if you please, to a member of the British Aristocracy who was, incidentally, a literary celebrity, a poet whose verse had won recognition in two continents.

As a matter of fact she was at that moment holding in her plump beringed hand a copy of his most recently published volume of verse. Yes, no doubt of it: *Rosemary for Rosencrantz*, author of *But Valour's Excrement*; and on the back of the weirdly designed jacket, in addition to the bit about the two continents, various laudatory snippets: '. . . trenchant satire . . . urgent symbolism . . . exotic imagery . . . foremost among the avant-garde . . . a young man to be watched . . .' And she turned to the fly-leaf and read once again with a glow of proprietary pride: Ma, With love etc, Lucas T.

Sitting in the cushioned window-seat and glancing across the placid fields now stripped of their screen of sugar cane to where a couple of miles away the control tower of the airport sparkled in the sun, Mrs Bush-Hall's accommodating bosom heaved in a swell of thanksgiving: her dearest ambition was on the way to fulfilment. She turned and directed her glance towards the interior of the too elaborately furnished room. At an old-fashioned desk littered with sheets of writing paper and envelopes, were bent two heads, one of them her future son-in-law's, pure Nordic gold, the other, her daughter's – and here a transient frown ruffled her sleek brow – well, she wished it didn't remind her so much of molasses froth.

But never mind that, she thought, never mind. It could pass for blonde, and it didn't seem to worry Lucas. She regarded his bowed head steadily, fondly. An English husband, no less, for her Pyrlene. Her bosom rose and fell again. This time the sigh reverberated.

The two heads were raised in enquiry.

'Was only thinkin', pet. You got down that master at the College? The one that does write poetry?'

'Lucas isn't impressed by his work, Mamma. He thinks it much too derivative. He says . . .'

'Oh stick him in, stick him in,' scowled the young man. 'He certainly won't be called upon to troll any of his tripe at the party.'

The girl giggled and the two heads were once more directed towards their task. And Mrs Bush-Hall continued to bask in the realisation of her good fortune. After all, Pyrlene wasn't exactly a beauty. Not much sex appeal there either: a little too flat at whatever angle you looked at her; but, perhaps for that very reason, she was a good girl. And intelligent too, no doubt about that: she could hold her own in conversation with anyone, even with such a world-famous figure as Lucas Traherne. Their conversations were a joy to listen to – not that she could understand much of what they were saying, of course: it was all so very highbrow. But she had no reason to be ashamed of her Pyrlene in that respect, and after marriage her looks would certainly improve; she had big bones. As for Lucas, what more could she have wished for! A great poet, a handsome, though somewhat skinny, young Englishman, and a close relative of a lord. Only, she wished he would take a little more care with his dress – those dirty white pumps of his were an eyesore – and that he would mix with the people of consequence in the island, join a few clubs as befitted his status, establish himself. But he just didn't seem to care for anything like that. Why, she'd had to beseech him to get a proper suit of clothes; had to take him to town, order it, pay for it even. Not that she minded; she loved making him little presents; had already bought him an expensive wrist watch; but these modern Englishmen were so casual, so careless of their personal appearance. Ah well, she'd show them what a B'adian woman could do.

The party had been her own idea. It wasn't to be a mere get-together of personal friends of theirs. Oh no, something on a much more socially grandiose scale. She had been to a British Council party once and had never forgotten it: all sorts of people, all the really important ones – various upper-class ladies and gentlemen, politicians, literary folks, artists and so on, headmasters and their wives, a member or two of the Legislative Council, English and American visitors to the island, the Lord Bishop, even the Governor (Acting) and his wife – all standing around casually in ever-shifting groups, with waiters bustling to and fro, and all chatting with one another in as friendly a manner as you could wish for, just as though there were no class-distinctions or prejudices or anything. A real eye-opener. So she was modelling her party along similar lines. Naturally there would be her own friends and acquaintances, among them the important members of the various associations to which she belonged and in which she played so prominent a part as a devoted apostle of social welfare: the ICU and the UCME, and the RSTU and the OHO and the AHA and the INOU. And of course there would be the nice American pastor of the NCSA; for Mrs Bush-Hall, although a nominal supporter of the C of E, was not averse to exploring the byways of religion which were offered in such profusion, and the New Church of Spiritual Automation was the most recent addition to their number. And her more intimate friends, her gentlemen friends especially . . . well, nearly all, for she would most certainly have to draw the line at Willoughby Watts. Much too coarse when he 'had in' his rum, and making passes at any attractive young woman within arm's length. A sudden vision of Willoughby Watts bestowing a good-natured smack on some upper-class bottom compelled her to question:

'You hasn't got that Willoughby on the list, has you, Pyrlie?'

'Certainly not, Mamma.'

Her composure restored, Mrs Bush-Hall resumed her reflections. No, come what might, she would never neglect her old friends, all men of substance who had in various capacities played an active part in her life: Jossie Ford, Big Boy Waterford, LeRoy DaCourcey . . . his wife, Lurleen, would have to come too, the old bitch, but no matter . . . and, of course, Audible Smart. Her own dear Audible. But in any case Audible would be foremost on the list of celebrities: a member of the House, with a ministerial job in the offing, the King, as he liked to describe himself in the papers, of Real Estate. A pity he had not viewed the advent of Lucas Traherne with favour. A blasted limey, he had dubbed him. But her insistence on Lucas's aristocratic connections had brought him round eventually; in fact they got on quite well together nowadays as the frequent replenishing of her two-gallon demijean bore witness. Yes, she was so glad that little difficulty had been smoothed over; she could never afford to lose her dear Audible's friendship. It was indeed mainly due to his good offices that she was now comfortably installed at this delightful old country house, 'The Frangipanis', away from all the noise and dust of Bridgetown.

How lovely the lawn would look beneath the festoons of coloured electric bulbs! And the frangipanis all in bloom too. Her glance strayed to the biggest of them all, its girth almost matching hers, its contorted branches forming a complicated pattern against the eggshell blue of the April sky. How she wished she could keep in mind those lines Lucas had composed especially for her, composed moreover, as a special favour to her, in rhyme. She would have to make the effort and learn them, those lines . . . how did they go?

Those knubbled elbows and arthritic knees
The something something among trees

and

Tittumty tumty years flow on
O arboreal Laocoon!

What a pity she couldn't memorise things like Pyrlene. Only a line or two here and there. O arboreal Laocoon! At first she had resented the reference to what she thought was 'coon', but Lucas had explained it so nicely. It was what they called a classical adhesion. Ah, what a thing education was! And to think that a poet had written that about *her* tree. She intended showing the poem to all the really important people at the party. Not ostentatiously, but casually like, when conversation flagged. 'My Lord Bishop, has you seen this?' or 'Speaking of frangipanis, Lady Graight . . .'

The name recalled her to a sense of the immediate.

'You write Lady Graight name yet, Pyrlene?'

'I doubt whether she'll be able to make it. She seldom goes anywhere nowadays. But we're sending her an invitation. And her secretary. Shall I tell you the invitees so far?'

Mrs Bush-Hall nodded and her daughter, scooping up a sheaf of envelopes, began:

'Mr and Mrs Pearson Porson, Major and Mrs Strokes, the Honourable and Mrs Boysie Scantlebury, Mr and Mrs Mauby Sorrell, Dr Dooms, Mr M. T. Vessle, MCP, Lady Graight, Miss Toothwaite, Mrs Fitzpitt, Mr and Mrs Celestial Barker, Miss Eurine Potts, Mrs Zimmerbloom . . .'

'Who she is?'

'The American sculptress, Mamma. Mr Talculm Fairenough, Mr and Mrs Smithbert Smith, Mr Audible Smart, MCP . . .'

'MCP,' repeated Lucas Traherne slowly with emphasis on the C. 'A curious thing, that. Today when colonialism is equated with serfdom and slavery, a relic of the barbarous past, your members of parliament still proudly insert that derogatory letter. Can you tell me why, Ma?'

But Mrs Bush-Hall had no explanation to offer. Nor had Pyrlene. 'I suppose they'll change it in time to MWIP, or something,' she offered.

Lucas Traherne held up his hands in horror, and Pyrlene continued:

'Mr Horatio Nelson, MA, the Reverend and Mrs Chirp, Mr Hathaway Withym, Sir Charles and Lady Charles . . .'

How proud Mrs Bush-Hall was at the recital of these notable names. She beamed.

And indeed she had every right to be proud of her achievement. She had every right to beam.

Born some forty-odd years ago in the most humble surroundings imaginable, she had, after many years of privation, married a retired and ageing stevedore; had seen him, after a few years of married life, impressively buried; and had then devoted herself to the rearing and education of her only child, and to the amassing, partly by means of her late husband's investments and partly by her own shrewdness, of quite a tidy income.

Mrs Bush-Hall was, as she liked to describe herself, a 'high brown', and must have been quite attractive in her youth. Her mother had been a poor negress who made her living, or most of it, by selling fruit. Rumour had it that her father was a white man, a foreigner, and Mrs Bush-Hall had always encouraged herself to believe that he was an Englishman. How else could she account for her passion for things English, for the possession of a pair of steely grey eyes, for her absorbing interest in the doings of the Royal Family? Yes, she was fully convinced it was the English blood that ran in her veins that, contrary to the reaction of the boys and girls in her neighbourhood, always brought her to a stiffly erect stance whenever the Police Band struck up God Save the King.

This conviction was a source of great satisfaction to her, and if any other circumstance was needed to strengthen it, was the fact that, when she reached her teens, she always felt much more at ease with English than with American sailors when a visiting man-of-war happened to be in the harbour.

But that was in her early days. She had attended a revivalist meeting one night and by the flaming light of hell-fire had been led to seek out the less demanding profession of needle-worker. By her twenty-fifth birthday she had acquired such an aura of respectability that Mr Molly Hall, the stevedore, who was a shrewd judge of character, had, after several abortive attempts to seduce her, proposed marriage. This was a great triumph for her, for Mr Hall was quite an important personality. He was a member of the parish vestry, owned no fewer than a dozen house properties, and, even in those days, a chauffeur-driven Ford. True, he was not altogether prepossessing: he was short, stout, of very dark complexion, well on in his sixties, and was more often than not rather the worse for liquor. But what were all these defects when offset by his wealth and respectability? Besides, his age was a factor in her favour.

So she, Maude Bush, spinster, had taken Mr M. Hall as her lawful wedded husband. It was not until after his death that she had adopted the hyphenated nomenclature by which she was distinguished from the many other Hall families in the neighbourhood of Hallscourt, Mr Hall's ornate residence in Bridgetown.

Mr Hall was delighted with his bride. Until then a bachelor, and a surprisingly childless one at that, it was his ambition that she should as swiftly as possible provide him with an heir, an ambition which it was said caused him within a few months of his marriage to take to the nuptial bed permanently as the result of an apoplectic seizure. This lack of an heir was his only regret, for his wife proved a most devoted nurse and soon showed such a grasp of his financial affairs that he appointed her his attorney and was relieved of all further worldly anxiety.

A short while before he died, however, there was some slight scandal that might have embarrassed a less integrated personality than his widow-to-be.

It was her love of the English and things English that occasioned the matter. She had, in the course of her transactions with a dry goods establishment, made the acquaintance of a commercial traveller from Birmingham. This acquaintance ripened into a more intimate relationship, for exactly eight months after the departure of the gentleman in question the child Pyrlene saw the light of day.

Not unnaturally, harsh things were said, but as Mr Hall made no comment (indeed he had lost the power of speech some time previously) and as there was no one to dispute the child's claim to legitimacy, Mrs Hall was quite pleased with the outcome of the affair, assuring all and sundry that the arrival of an heir, though female, was the long-deferred answer to her husband's prayer, and that now she would not be at all surprised if he departed in peace, which he did shortly afterwards.

One hundred and three cars followed Mr Hall's mortal remains to the cemetery, and everyone allowed that his widow had done all in her power to make the occasion a success.

She was now extremely well off. In addition to the late Mr Hall's title deeds and bank balance there was his accumulation of old gold: the various rings, brooches and other bits of antique jewellery in the japanned box under his bed were worth at least, she was assured, well over two thousand pounds.

She was not surprised therefore to find herself, after the correct time had elapsed, besieged by a variety of suitors. She had always been led to believe that the two essential prerequisites to happiness were love and money: having experienced a surfeit of the former in her youth, she was in no mind to sacrifice her enjoyment of the latter by sharing it with any gentleman of her acquaintance. Not that she was averse to their attentions. A chosen few who could help her swell her bank balance by judicious advice or assistance were encouraged to call at Hallscourt; and these callers would often prolong their calls until the early hours of the next day.

But even these indiscretions were abruptly terminated shortly after Pyrlene's fifth birthday. Until that time the child had been for the most part a source of annoyance: she suffered from almost every ailment to which young children are prone and would frequently cause her mother to leave her bed at most inopportune moments.

And then one morning her mother discovered her spelling out the words in the *Sunday Advocate*. This was a revelation. She was the mother of a genius, of a potential Barbados Scholar! All her energy must now be devoted to the education of this prodigy. Everything must be done to ensure success. The best schools. The best home training and influence. Those protracted calls must cease.

And so began the educational progress of Pyrlene, and, incidentally, of Mrs Bush-Hall; for from expensive private school on to Princess Royal College the pair would tackle the homework problem together; and thus the older student was introduced to the hitherto unknown world of letters – *Dick Whittington*, *The Golden Fleece*, *Little Women*. It was unfortunate for her that Shakespeare made such an early appearance on the curriculum of Princess Royal: blank verse left her mind in a similar condition; so very wisely she allowed her daughter to continue on her own. But having acquired the habit of reading, Mrs Bush-Hall was not to be denied: there were thrillers, romances, westerns to provide her with the entertainment and excitement she craved. Besides, as she would often remark, 'reading is the hallmark of the truly cultured person'.

Meanwhile Pyrlene was making reasonably satisfactory progress. She was duly promoted from form to form. But by the time she reached the upper school it was obvious that she was not of the material of which scholars are made: in her first important exam she failed in almost every subject.

Her mother was furious. Her life's work had been in vain. Poor Pyrlene's life became insupportable. Her woebegone appearance and frequent uncontrolled bursts of sobbing became a topic of comment at school. Her form mistress, Miss Toothwaite, an Englishwoman who had become a long-established fixture at Princess Royal, had questioned her. As a result one afternoon Miss Toothwaite had accompanied Pyrlene to Hallscourt.

'Barbados Scholarships aren't the aim and end of education, you know, Mrs Bush-Hall. In any case, despite Pyrlene's failure in certain subjects, her results in English were outstanding.' (Miss Toothwaite had been English mistress for years.) 'A greater future lies in store for your daughter.'

What this future was Miss Toothwaite did not choose to disclose, but in Mrs Bush-Hall's imagination the words of the gaunt grey-haired Englishwoman (at school she was known as Duppy) were fraught with prophetic assurance. Her doubt and anger were dispelled. Hope was reborn. She embraced Miss Toothwaite and wept unrestrainedly on her shoulder and invited her to stay on to dinner. Mrs Bush-Hall was an excellent cook, everyone was happy, and Miss Toothwaite spent a most rewarding evening. She was entreated to come soon again. Entreaty was hardly necessary: she came often. Very soon she was invited to Hallscourt for weekends, and when soon afterwards the removal to 'The Frangipanis' took place, she would sometimes spend the greater part of her vacation there. The friendship proved mutually beneficial. Miss Toothwaite was able to add to her meagre savings and attenuated frame and Mrs Bush-Hall to her cultural development. For Miss Toothwaite was convinced that such a dynamic personality had much to offer the community; so she encouraged her with the help of Mr Audible Smart's influence to enter the field of Social Welfare. She became a member of one of the many organisations devoted to the cause. She was congratulated on her ability, her zeal. She became a member of another association. And another. Then several. She sat on various committees. Her circle of acquaintance widened. Her photograph appeared in the press. She gave tea parties. Her tea parties, with Miss Toothwaite always present to disseminate a modicum of culture, were minor social events. And Pyrlene, relieved from the terrors of her mother's now averted ambition, made satisfactory amends by obtaining passes in no fewer than three subjects at her next public examination and left school (she was now nineteen) to pursue a course of study of the more esoteric modern poets whose ranks she hoped to join some day when her mother allowed her to emigrate to the wider literary field of London.

And then Lucas Traherne appeared on the scene. One afternoon Miss Toothwaite's moribund two-seater wheezed up the drive at 'The Frangipanis'. A young man, a stranger, was driving. Miss Toothwaite dashed up the wide stone steps breathless with excitement and the young man followed at a leisurely pace. He was windblown and dishevelled, his clothes were far from clean, a pair of pale blue eyes glittered from a rawly-pink face; he had a lean and hungry look. In short, he might have been one of those merchant seamen who prowled the streets of Bridgetown.

By the time he had reached the broad verandah, Miss Toothwaite had performed her act of introduction. She had gone for a sea-bathe. She had met him on the beach. They had got talking. And he was no other . . . why, they had been reading his *Rosemary for Rosencrantz* only last week . . . than Lucas Traherne.

Soon, stretched in a berbice chair with a tall rum and ginger at hand, he was relating his odyssey. He was touring the Caribbean. Writing. He liked Barbados. In fact, he liked it best of all the islands. How long was he staying? That depended – and here he looked around appraisingly – if he could find a less expensive boarding-house. Poets couldn't afford the best hotels.

Next morning he moved in. A small suitcase arrived with him. That had been six months ago.

He had on more than one occasion offered to pay for his keep, that is to say, to pay when a certain cheque from his publishers arrived. But the cheque had failed to appear, and Mrs Bush-Hall had been forced to console herself with the thought that the intention was as good as the deed. Besides, it was a privilege to entertain such a distinguished guest. Moreover he was so entertaining, so companionable, so easily pleased, so useful even. He shared her enthusiasm for thrillers; regaled them with all sorts of stories – stories of the eccentricities of his illustrious family, bawdy stories of various personalities of the stage, screen and literary world, shocking stories of political intrigue and dissimulation; pottered about in the garden and gave her invaluable hints about her roses, was delighted with the unfamiliar tropical blooms and exceedingly impressed by her collection of anthuriums (even more impressed by the collection of antique jewellery in the japanned box under the bed); often gave a hand in the kitchen; went marketing for her two or three times a week; and, when she broached the idea of a new car, saw after all the complicated business transactions and drove it home himself, a shining Jaguar. True, he would attend none of her tea parties, nor did he display the slightest interest in social welfare, but he was most affable to Miss Toothwaite despite her inability to cope with the more obscurantist and obscene of his poems, hail-fellow-well-met with the gregarious Audible, quite filial in his deportment to his dear Ma, and to Pyrlene he was most attentive. Indeed, after the arrival of the Jaguar, the couple would often disappear after dinner until the early hours of the next morning; and in spite of her daughter's repeated assurance that they spent the time discussing the problems and intricacies of modern verse, it was at this stage that Mrs Bush-Hall determined that he should state his intentions.

No matter how famous, how well-connected a young man he might be, the honour of the Bush-Halls was at stake. She wasn't going to have any monkey-business where the reputation of her only daughter was concerned.

He was watering the anthuriums when she put the pertinent question to him bluntly.

He shook a reproving finger at her. 'No wonder you are prey to these fearful imaginings, Ma, surrounded as you are' (and here he took in the tiers of lilies with a wide sweep of his arm) 'by all these travesties of floral phallism. But I can appreciate a mother's feelings and concern. My dear Ma' (approaching her and pinching her cheek) 'I thought all that was understood between us long ago. When do you propose announcing the engagement?'

And in spite of his sustaining a number of minor contusions by being propelled backwards into a nest of flowerpots by the exuberance of Mrs Bush-Hall's embrace, there was great joy at 'The Frangipanis' that day.

The Day broke fair and cloudless, Mrs Bush-Hall having consulted every available almanac to ensure this end. She had been up and about before dawn, and had been on her legs every moment since. All the multifarious preparations had fallen upon her, for Lucas had had to go to town in the car immediately after breakfast on important but unspecified business, Miss Toothwaite was busy at school, Audible involved in some political activity, and Pyrlene hadn't been at all well lately, especially during the morning hours; but then, once the preliminaries had been accomplished in fitting style, the wedding need not be too long delayed. It would be a quiet one: she had promised Lucas he would not have to undergo *two* such social trials.

A day of hard work it had been for her: arranging the floral decorations; giving instructions to the men from the electric company about the illuminations; seeing that the caterers had sent everything; popping in and out of the kitchen to supervise all that was going on there; keeping a wary eye on the criss-crossing ropes from the two marquees erected between the house and the lawn and upon all the strange men wandering about the house and grounds, and the consequent checking and rechecking of the knives, forks, spoons, etc; arranging the few dozen chairs in apparently haphazard fashion about the lawn (she had wanted to order two hundred and fifty, but Miss Toothwaite had reminded her that too many chairs at a function of this sort would only engender a crystallisation in the circulation, and Lucas, less elegantly, that it wasn't going to be another of her bloody tea parties); pointing out to the gardener and the boy who ran errands just how the parking of the cars was to be controlled . . . yes, it had been a day of hard work, not without its petty exasperations too. Major Strokes had telephoned to state he was laid low with an attack of ptomaine poisoning; Audible had warned her that Willoughby Watts had no intention of foregoing a freeness for lack of such a trifle as an invitation; one of the young men from the village who had been pressed into service had had an epileptic seizure in the WC and old Dr Dooms had had to be summoned; a stray dog had made off with one of the baked turkeys; and, to cap it all, Lucas had just telephoned to say that something – nothing very serious, he had been at pains to tell her – had gone wrong with the car and that he would have to return by taxi.

Such a day! Nearly half-past five. Invitations had been issued for six-thirty. She would have to wash and dress. And the question of dress had caused her some exasperation too. She had wanted to appear in her most elaborate and expensive gown and displaying almost every bit of jewellery she possessed; but Lucas had been firm. 'That sort of thing just isn't done, Ma. You don't want all these people to think you're trying to make them look insignificant. Something simple. And just one ring and the little necklace I gave you. Remember now.'

She would certainly wear the necklace, even though it did look rather cheap; but she had been thrilled at this unexpected gift, and she consoled herself with the thought that one who had attended garden parties at Windsor should know best.

She fingered the little gilt chain wistfully. She hadn't removed it since he had clasped it on a week ago. For only a week ago the long-expected cheque from his publishers had arrived. True, it was not quite what he had been counting upon: only a matter of some twenty pounds, and there were so many things to be done with it. His old suitcase had completely burst asunder, and he had bought one of those lovely ones they used for air travel; he had run up quite a bill for cigarettes at the village shop; and he had so wanted to buy that beautiful engagement ring at Snuyder's he'd set his heart on. He'd even offered to pay what was left of the cheque on account. But paying two pounds ten on a $500 engagement ring would have been quite out of the question, so she had advanced the money (five per cent off for cash) and with the two pounds ten – or rather the better part of it – he had purchased the necklace especially for her. She sighed tenderly at the recollection, and, as her bosom heaved, again glimpsed for a fleeting moment that delicate token of his esteem.

Calling out last-minute instructions to everyone within earshot, she climbed the stairs slowly. She hoped her legs would last out the night. Pyrlene, in the next room busily engaged in putting the finishing touches to a poem of hers which she hoped Lucas might, considering the theme and the occasion, read, was routed from her occupation and told to keep a close eye on the liquor now that the head-waiter had arrived and to hustle Lucas into his clothes the moment he returned from town, and then Mrs Bush-Hall made ready for her night of nights.

Her night of nights! That primary phase of her obligation as hostess accomplished, the reception of her guests, she had withdrawn to the topmost stair of the verandah, and from this point of vantage was contemplating with satisfaction the pulsating scene before her.

She was dressed in a white satin gown that displayed her rounded figure perhaps a little too bumpily, but Lucas, arriving at the very last moment, had approved. Had approved also of the three salmon-coloured frangipani blossoms in her hair, and had, on second thoughts, granted her permission to wear another of her rings. The rest she had been compelled to deposit regretfully in her jewel case. And Lucas had whispered to her that she reminded him of a very famous duchess indeed, a duchess of his acquaintance.

Lucas had returned only just in time. There had been a slight accident; he had had to leave the car in town, but it would be all right by tomorrow. He had been unusually agitated, but her reminder that men were prone to attacks of nerves at such crises had seemed to have restored his composure. He got dressed quickly, joined Pyrlene and herself in greeting the early arrivals, and had been quite charming to them.

What more could even a duchess have wished for? Everything had combined to make the occasion astonishingly perfect. As she gazed out into the night she noted that even the stars in their courses – and she could never remember having seen such a profusion of them before – were obviously giving her of their best, the lawn with its festoons of multi-coloured electric bulbs re-echoed loftier splendours, and the lights from the airport, too, winked unqualified approval in her direction. And all the guests, the two hundred odd of them, were so completely, so indubitably at their ease. Their chatter and laughter were wafted up to her, a duchess upon her dais, almost drowning the delicate drone of the scarlet-coated steel band which had been instructed to play only the lightest of classical music until eight o'clock, when the buffet supper would be served and the engagement announced.

How happy she was, how proud of it all – the weather, the stars, the lights, the gay assembly! How delightful everyone had been! Everyone, including Sir Charles Charles, that paragon of the old Barbadian order about whose acceptance of the invitation she had entertained some misgiving. How very gracious he and his wife, Lady Emma, had been to her: 'Charmed, charmed to meet you, Mrs Bush-Hall,' he had boomed, and had somehow managed to infuse into his greeting the fact that he had only at that moment achieved a life-long desire. Breeding will always tell, she thought: good old B'adian blood. She was more than ever proud of her birthright. Little England and Big England for ever.

Audible, very slim and very elegant in his fawn tropicals, mounted the steps and joined her.

'Ain't it all too good to be true, Audie?' she murmured.

Audible grunted approval. 'You certainly giving them one hell of a good time, Maudie. But why you up here all by your one? Where Pyrlene and Lucas?'

She pointed them out where they stood in the centre of a little knot of people whom Pyrlene had previously referred to as 'the literati'. 'I going jine them now,' she said.

The two of them walked down the steps to the lawn.

Smiles greeted her everywhere. Mrs Zimmerbloom, the American sculptress, again assured her what a wonderful time she was having and admired her cute frangipani-coiffure, the Beethoven Smalls were effusively appreciative of the pleasantly modulated effect of the steel band, the Honourable Boysie Scantlebury congratulated her in his warmest and moistest tone on the excellence of her whisky, Mrs Orgie Wilde, the secretary of the HIYA, was moved to ecstatic ejaculations of 'Divine, my dear, too too divine' as she caught sight of her, Mr Hathaway Withym could not forbear introducing her for a second time to his most recently acquired friend, a young German, Herr Panzi, and even Lurleen DaCourcey felt it incumbent upon her to confess it was as good as an evening at Government House.

Audible wandered off in search of an elderly American who had earlier in the evening expressed a desire to purchase a property somewhere near the ocean. Mrs Bush-Hall joined the party of literati.

'All o' you still talking poetry, I suppose?'

'And what could be more essentially worth our while?' replied the eldest of the group, bowing acknowledgement. This was Mr Pearson Porson, an Englishman who had been shipped to the colonies many years ago to seek his fortune and had found it in the person of the daughter of a wealthy planter. Since that far-off time he had never done a stroke of work but was regarded as a great authority on every conceivable subject.

'That's right, Mrs Bush-Hall,' added another, a young journalist who was responsible for very occasional verse in his paper. And a third, the young schoolmaster to whose presence at the party Lucas had at first objected, chimed in, 'We're all now anxiously awaiting Mr Traherne's magnum opus, his epithalamium, to which this wonderful party,' with a sweeping wafture of his rum-and-ginger, 'would seem to be its most fitting prolegomenon.'

Not quite sure of the meaning of the intended compliment, Mrs Bush-Hall could only smile and glance at Lucas. He was scowling his darkest. 'Yes,' she ventured haltingly, 'we hope so. We hope so.'

Mr Pearson Porson came to the rescue. 'I was just saying, Mrs Bush-Hall,' he asserted in his most pontifical manner, 'that Mr Traherne can hardly have failed to observe the exquisite charm of our local place names, so English, so inspiring, so fraught with the mellow tradition of the centuries: Foursquare, Strong Hope, Mount Standfast, Providence, Venture, Boarded Hall . . .'

'And don't forget the purely B'adian touch,' interrupted the journalist. 'Six Men's and Pie Corner and Jack-in-the-Box Gully . . .'

'And Jack-My-Nanny Gap and Penny-Hole and Cat's Castle . . .' added the schoolmaster.

'And,' Lucas interpolated acidly, breaking his hitherto glowering silence, 'above all, don't let us forget the most inspiring of the lot, Sweet Bottom.' And, turning abruptly on his heel, he strode away followed by Pyrlene.

Mr Pearson Porson drew in his lips primly. The others, after a spell of indecision, made clucking noises of disapproval. Mrs Bush-Hall essayed a conciliatory 'He will have his little joke, you know', but Mr Pearson Porson's lips retained their set contour and his stare was stony. She thought it best to follow the retreating figure of Pyrlene. Lucas had gone on ahead and had disappeared indoors. 'Pyrlene!' she called. Pyrlene stopped and Mrs Bush-Hall caught up with her.

'Why Lucas had to go and make old Porson vex, na?'

'Mamma, you just won't understand. You know how Lucas hates parties and all this social fuss. You know it was only after days of persuasion we could get him to agree to this. And you know how most of these people irritate him, especially that pompous old ass, Porson. *And* that schoolmaster. Well he has just blown up, that's all. He is in the most frightful temper. He has gone to his room and he says no one must disturb him until we're actually ready to announce the engagement.'

'But, Pyrlie, what people going say? And how I going know the exack time to send for him?'

Pyrlene shrugged her chiffon-covered shoulders. 'All I know is you'd better not trouble him when he's like this. He'll take a little time to cool off. He'll be all right. Don't hurry things. Start serving at eight as arranged. I'll go and bring him down about a quarter past. It's not even half-past seven yet.'

And Mrs Bush-Hall had to be content with that. After all, she reflected, it wasn't likely that he would be missed among all these people. Indeed, they all seemed to be enjoying themselves more than ever: the chatter and laughter had increased, the waiters were in great demand, the steel band seemed to be jazzing up some of the light classicals.

She caught sight of Miss Toothwaite. Miss Toothwaite had been delegated to entertain the strictly scholastic element, the various headmasters and headmistresses, and she was performing her duty with distinction. She had collected them all together, and from their sustained gurgles and guffaws, had apparently been plying them with drinks and a number of Lucas's bawdy stories.

The literati had dissolved into units. Mr Pearson Porson was gesticulating to two old ladies, the journalist had joined a politically inclined group, the schoolmaster had disappeared. A withered elderly lady enmeshed in a cocoon of mauve voile approached her and seized her arm. It was Miss Twaddelle, the founder and president of the ICU. 'My dear Mrs Bush-Hall, what a beautiful party! And what a fine young man! So reserved, so well-tempered, so very English! And your dear daughter: how sweet she looks tonight! Ah, well she may to have captured the heart of so famous a person. And, just imagine: I've met every single member of our committee already!' Chirping gaily and sipping her rum-and-ginger, she melted into the crowd.

As she moved slowly across the lawn (how her legs were aching!) many others accosted her and had a few words with her: Sir Charles expressed his appreciation of the most delightful evening, the Smithbert Smiths were enchanted, Mr Gray Whitefoot was enraptured, Mr Horatio Nelson, MA, could find no words to express his ecstatic frame of mind; and all were equally congratulatory on her acquisition of so fine, so famous a son-in-law.

All this cheered her up a bit, but, God, she was tired. On her legs all day. As she moved around to a far corner of the lawn, she espied a couple of chairs which she remembered having placed in that secluded spot in the event of just such a contingency. She manoeuvred her way to them skilfully without being seen, and flopping down and removing her shoes, she occupied both of them to best advantage.

From where she sat she could hear bits of conversation all around her. To her left, some enthusiasts were noisily selecting the next West Indian eleven, and there was great controversy. W. W. W. Pelter, himself a coming fast bowler, was maintaining stoutly that what the team needed was a spearhead attack of five fast bowlers. What did it matter if such an experiment had never yet been tried? So much the better . . . To her right, the American pastor of the New Church of Spiritual Automation seemed to be expounding the tenets of his sect to a chosen few. She could hear '. . . for not only is the human body a machine, the soul too is a machine, if you come to think of it, a mechanical psyche motivated by the Great Mechanic . . .' Immediately behind her, the future of the Federation was being debated. Mr Celestial Barker appeared to be voicing the consensus of opinion in stating that complete and absolute independence could be easily achieved if the hat were to be circulated among those nations who had more wealth than was morally good for them.

Hearing all these interesting points of view and not being compelled either to listen very carefully or to say anything in reply was extremely soothing. She could afford to forget Lucas and supper and everything else for a few moments. She stretched out her legs still further . . .

Mrs Bush-Hall slept.

She was being rocked to and fro violently to the accompaniment of a prolonged shriek emanating from countless souls in despairing agony. As she struggled back to consciousness she became aware that the shriek was only the accustomed sound of a jet plane leaving the airport; it took her a little longer to realise that Pyrlene was responsible for the violence to her person.

'What the hell you think you doing, Pyrlene?' she enquired testily.

Pyrlene continued her shaking. 'Wake up, Mamma, wake up!'

'Stop that damn foolishness. You ain't see I wake up, girl?'

'Mamma, Mamma, you know what time it is? I been looking for you for the last half-hour. We had to start supper . . .'

Mrs Bush-Hall was wide awake now. 'What time it is?'

'Nearly half-past eight. And . . . and . . . I can't find Lucas anywhere.'

'Can't find Lucas?'

Pyrlene sank on to the chair now vacated by her mother's feet and sobbed: 'Nowhere at all, at all.'

Mrs Bush-Hall slipped on her shoes and stood up. Her fatigue had vanished. 'How you meaning you can't find Lucas?'

Pyrlene continued sobbing. 'Can't find him. Went to his room. Went to call him at quarter past eight. Wasn't there. All his clothes gone. His suitcase. Everything.'

From the far distance the sound of the retreating plane drilled a terrible thought into Mrs Bush-Hall's consciousness.

'Gone?'

'Me and Audible been searching everywhere. Didn't want to tell nobody. Couldn't find you. Why you had to go and get los' way so?'

'Come, chile,' said her mother, pulling her to her feet. It was useless reproaching herself for having dozed off. Only that terrible thought, persistent, boring its way into her brain. 'Come lewwe go and see. Where Audible is now?'

But Pyrlene did not know, and they set out across the lawn. Progress was difficult. They had to push their way through little knots of people, some of whom wanted to engage her in conversation. Willoughby Watts, who had evidently arrived late, slipped an arm around her: 'Hey, Maudie, like my invitation must be get los' in the post.' She ignored him. He could be dealt with later.

They found Audible in the hall at the telephone. He was on the point of replacing the receiver and he turned to them with a set face and much profanity. 'You know what, Maudie? That goddam limey cut and run. I now ring the airport. The sonofabitch gone by that plane that just lef'.'

Mrs Bush-Hall did not speak. She grabbed Audible by the arm and pulled him upstairs. With that thought now in complete possession, she made straight for her bedroom. She opened her jewel case. She motioned to Audible to pull out the box from beneath the bed. Yes. Only a few bits of imitation jewellery now adorned the case; the japanned box had been rifled.

'If I could only ketch the thieving bastard,' Audible almost sobbed, 'if I could only *ketch* him . . .'

'He have the engagement ring too?'

Pyrlene, a dumb heap on the floor, nodded assent.

For a few moments no one spoke.

Then Audible made for the door.

'Where you going, Audie?'

'To call the police.'

'You isn't doing nothing of the sort. Ring police for what? They got planes too? You keep your tail quiet, you hear, Audible Smart? This business concerning me. What *I* los', *I* los'. Nobody else. I got to think.'

A strange scene it was. Outside the music and the noise of the party louder than ever; within the room the three figures. Pyrlene sobbing, Audible blaspheming, Mrs Bush-Hall thinking. Thinking calmly, coherently, lucidly. She had been tricked, completely tricked. And in the very audacity of the trickery she found something she could, however ruefully, admire. Only Lucas could have done a thing like that. It was strange, he had made a complete fool of her, and yet . . . she bore him no malice. She had lost out. Lost maybe six or seven thousand dollars, lost the son-in-law of her dreams, everything she had planned, had hoped for, had boasted about . . . and yet . . . She liked Lucas. She had enjoyed those months of his stay more than any other period of time she could remember. He was the only man she had really ever *liked.* If it had been her instead of Pyrlene . . .

She glanced down at the sobbing girl on the floor. At least, all going well, there should be at 'The Frangipanis' in a few months' time a scion of English aristocracy. She would have to be content with that. And with her memories. And should she now go downstairs and announce to them all that Lucas was just a common thief and that she, Maude Bush-Hall, was the damnedest fool in Barbados? She could see the faces: the white faces, apparently sympathetic and scandalised, but smirking inwardly, old Sir Charles 'That's the sort of Englishman they export nowadays'; and the dark faces, goggle-eyed, drinking it all in, Willoughby Watts's fat grin, 'English son-in-law! Serve her damn well right, playing she is some society great dame.' She wasn't going to have *that.* Nobody was going to have the pleasure of seeing *her* spirit broken. Of course they would eventually hear the truth, but not from her. Not tonight. Not on her night of nights. What was it he had said? Like a duchess. A duchess . . .

'Stop that snivelling, Pyrlene, and get up. Come with me. We going downstairs.'

'But what you going do?' questioned Audible.

'You go and round up the folks and tell them to gather in front the verandah. I got something to tell them.'

But something was worrying Audible. 'What I want to know is how he get the money to pay his fare. He couldn't give them no ring nor brooch nor nothing like that. And I know he didn't have a blasted blind cent.'

Pyrlene came to life. 'The Jag! The Jag! I bet he sell the Jag!'

But if Mrs Bush-Hall heard, she took no notice. She was already on her way.

For the past half-hour Miss Toothwaite had been feeling rather upset. Not only had she been steadily sipping away at far too many rum-and-gingers, but she could not understand the prolonged delay. Dear Maudie was always so efficient, so punctual. She glanced around. Everyone was becoming restless. And the wind was growing chilly. And those wretched calypsoes. Over and over. Where was Maudie? Whatever could have happened?

It was then that she observed that everyone was moving forward to the stone stairway leading up to the verandah. Mr Smart seemed to be directing operations. With the assistance of the arm of one of the headmasters, she discovered she could move forward, although not too quickly. So the announcement was to be made at last. But where was the young man? From her point of observation at the back of the crowd she could glimpse Pyrlene, all alone and almost hidden by one of the stone uprights, and Mrs Bush-Hall standing on the topmost stair. She couldn't help thinking how imposing she looked, how very dignified. Not in the least bit nervous, except that she was toying with that ridiculous little necklace Lucas had given her. What was she saying? There was a good stiff breeze blowing, and Miss Toothwaite, whose hearing was not particularly good, could catch only a few words here and there.

Mrs Bush-Hall was thanking them all for their acceptance of her invitation and for attending her party. She appreciated their presence. They all knew the object of the gathering . . . She was speaking in her best committee voice, but was occasionally in difficulty with certain rules of concord. Dear, dear, she'd have to remind her again about the agreement of the verb with its subject . . . What was she saying now?

'. . . one hour ago Mr Traherne receive a cable from home. It going shock all-you to hear . . . his dear mother dying . . . express a wish to see him before she pass away . . . no time to lose . . . what we could do? . . . no matter how much we want him to stay . . . a mother's dying wish . . . me and Pyrlene had to decide fast . . . Mr Smart here . . . arrangements . . . phone the airport . . . thank God . . . in time . . . plane . . . just gone . . .'

Good gracious, what a calamity! How very unfortunate for everyone concerned. Miss Toothwaite communicated her distress to Dr Phorpous, the headmaster of St Swynethold's, on whose arm she was still depending. But Dr Phorpous replied quite unexpectedly and rather callously, she thought, 'Anyway, Miss Toothwaite, we've enjoyed a very pleasant evening. That turkey and ham was excellent.'

Mrs Bush-Hall was still speaking and Miss Toothwaite caught the last words quite clearly: '. . . and Mr Traherne beg me to say how sorry he was he didn't have the chance to wish all-you goodbye.'

Then she appeared to give a little sob and to clutch at her bosom. 'Poor Maudie,' thought Miss Toothwaite. 'I hope she doesn't go and have a stroke or something.'

But it was only the necklace that had come apart.

The broken chain was still dangling from her hand when Miss Toothwaite, with the continued assistance of Dr Phorpous's arm, struggled up the steps to wish her goodnight. They were almost the last to leave. Dr Phorpous had not been able to forgo the whisky and soda he had ordered some time previously, and the band was doing its best with God Save the Queen when they reached the top of the steps. She had wanted to say a few words, words of sympathy – she hardly knew what, but at that moment something had happened, something she couldn't understand, something that was to puzzle her for another few days. For Dr Phorpous, bending gallantly over Mrs Bush-Hall's proffered hand, had whispered, 'As an Englishman, I want to thank you very humbly for your magnificent gesture in defence of the Old Country'; and what had puzzled her even more was that Mrs Bush-Hall had winked, actually winked, at him, and had replied in her most gracious manner, 'Ah, Dr Phorpous, *noblesse oblige*, you know, *noblesse oblige*.'

The Diaries

The diaries had been packed away in an old bookcase in the storeroom, and well over half-a-dozen years had elapsed before I took the trouble to do more than glance cursorily through a few of them. The angular, spidery handwriting wasn't very inviting, and the entries appeared for the most part to consist of either household accounts or of the customary commonplace jottings in which diaries abound: *To church. Rev G. gave a grand sermon*, or, *William down with cough & cold & fever again*, or, *Whytes spent the eve with us. Whist. Mrs W. very poor player*, and so on and so on.

But perhaps I should first explain how the diaries had come into my possession, and this entails a few words about their compiler.

The late Mrs Selina Casper had been something of a character. Always dressed in black and completely disdaining the dictates of fashion, hers had been a familiar figure in Bridgetown some thirty years ago. On Saturday mornings especially her somewhat forbidding figure could be seen stalking through Broad Street as she went about her shopping with her chauffeur close behind her laden with an assortment of parcels and bundles.

At that time I was one of the junior partners of the firm of Dryden & Milbank, solicitors, where regularly once a month she would call and have lengthy sessions with old Mr Dryden, the then senior partner. There would be some investment to be considered; for Mrs Casper was pretty well off as we all knew.

She must have been in her thirties when I first became acquainted with her, although the old-fashioned costume which she affected added at least ten years to her appearance. Pale, tight-lipped, sharp-nosed, her heavy hair braided severely beneath a grotesque sort of bonnet, she would march into the office, transact her business with Mr Dryden, and depart without so much as a 'good morning' to anyone else, although she seemed to pierce us through with those cold steely-blue eyes of hers.

As the years passed, her visits to the city became less frequent, and we saw her but seldom. By this time she had deigned to become aware of my presence, especially after Mr Dryden's death, and eventually it was to me that she would turn for advice. Her ruling passion seemed to be acquisition of money, and more money. I was never able to understand the reason for this. She lived alone now, had no relatives or friends, and the old house where she had lived since the early days of her first marriage was in sad need of repair.

On all the occasions on which I had met her, her manner had always been self-assured and business-like. I had never known her to gossip or to say more than was absolutely necessary. Nor had I ever known her to smile, and no wonder. Except in money-matters, life had dealt very harshly with her. Her first husband, who had sold his sugar estates at the right time during the first world war, and to whom she was indebted for the bulk of her fortune, had died after a brief illness. Her second husband, after three years of married life and alcoholism, had fallen downstairs one night and injured himself fatally. And William, her only son by her first husband, had committed suicide. He had been a shy, introspective youth, and had been subject to fits of depression and melancholia. His mother had never recovered from this tragedy; thereafter she seemed to have lost all interest in life, except, as I have mentioned, that of the acquisition of money.

And then, some six years ago, she herself had been knocked down by a speeding cane lorry and killed on the spot.

About a month before her death, she had summoned me to her home. I had always been puzzled that, despite her considerable wealth, she had never made a will. This was what she now wanted to do. I was shocked at her appearance: she had wasted away to a mere frame of skin and bone. Her manner, too, had altered. She was no longer the self-assured person I had known. Her hands trembled violently, and she would start at the slightest sound. Only her cold, steely-blue eyes served to remind me of the woman I had known. As there were no surviving relatives, she wanted to leave all her money to some charitable institution where it would be of the greatest service to the poor and needy. What would I suggest? I was surprised, but I made my suggestion which was accepted. The will was drawn up, and I departed.

As executor, I was to receive the sum of one hundred pounds – and her diaries. 'You may find them amusing,' she said in her grim business-like manner of old.

There were several bundles of them, each securely tied up with white tape.

Well, it wasn't until a couple of weeks ago that I thought I would do a bit of cleaning up. I was taking a brief holiday; the old storeroom needed repair; the bookcase was in a sad condition, and its contents equally so – most of them riddled with moth; and I thought I would salvage what I could – most of them forgotten novels and paperbacks – and throw away the rest.

The diaries had suffered rather badly: some of the bundles had become completely welded together in solid blocks and others so honeycombed with bookworm that the handwriting was almost undecipherable.

I was about to pitch the lot into a corner with the rest of the litter, when the tape around one of the bundles gave way, and the books fell to the floor. One of them happened to lie open, and, as I picked it up, I glanced at the entry on the page before me.

There was just the one entry. It read: *1924. Dec. 11. Nathan* (that was the name of her first husband, I remembered, Nathan Morant) *buried today at St Aubyn's. What a relief.*

How very odd, I thought. I read the entry again. There could be no doubt about it: the word relief was underlined, three definite (though faded), lines in red ink.

I pulled a chair up to the bookcase, sat down, and proceeded to read through as much of the diary as had escaped the onslaught of moth and worm. But nowhere could I find anything that might explain this strange entry. William, her son, had been *down with his customary trouble* on three or four occasions; she had won a sweepstake of one hundred and thirty-two dollars at the races; one of the servants had been dismissed for stealing. Nathan, who hadn't been feeling well for some time, had contracted enteritis and, after a fortnight's illness, had died. His property had been left to his son when he came of age, and she had been appointed sole trustee. And that was all.

I then continued reading such of the contents of the next two years' diaries as I could. Except for summaries of investments and the daily commonplace notes, nothing; and those of the next three years were in such a condition of disintegration that it was quite impossible to decipher even a single entry.

I had better luck, however, with those of the next two years, 1930 and 1931. Her second husband, George Casper, had, I knew, died in the former year, and I was wondering what comment I should find on *his* interment.

I read on avidly, and, as I did so, I could hardly believe the evidence of my own eyes.

I have selected a few entries from the diary of 1930 which, brief as they are, will sufficiently serve to summarise the sequence of the events which had so astounded me.

I should mention here that almost all the entries were defaced to some extent. Where there can be no possible occasion of doubt, I have supplied the missing letters or words.

And so –

May 16. Geo drunk again . . . car smashed . . .

June 22. Employed chauffeur today . . . John Jackson . . . very prepossessing young man . . .

Aug. 2. . . . own bedroom now . . . drunk for the past week . . . intolerable . . .

Aug. 13. . . . tried to enter my room last night . . . protection . . . J. will now sleep on the premises . . .

Aug. 18. . . . dreadful condition . . . tried to break down my door . . . J. so understanding, so strong . . .

Oct. 11. . . . the drunken fool will never suspect . . .

Nov. 7. . . . if only the men I had married were half so . . .

Nov. 10. . . . think he is suspicious . . . we must do something . . . should be quite easy to . . .

Nov. 18. . . . all arranged now . . .

And then –

Nov. 30. . . . widow once again. Ha ha!

Dec. 2. . . . over at last . . . accidental death . . . medical evidence that blow on the back of his head . . . lucky thought of the banister . . . J. rather scared but magnificent giving evidence . . . little William sleeps so soundly . . . plus those pills . . .

Dec. 31. . . . should be quite happy now . . . but William very trying . . . so morose and selfish . . . acts so strangely . . . at times I wonder . . . in his father's family . . .

I have included this last entry in view of what happened much later.

I cannot bring myself to quote any of the numerous, and ironically enough, perhaps the most legible of all, entries from the diary of the following year. All I shall state is that the fervid devourer of erotica would find much to entertain him, and that, recalling the staid and puritanical demeanour of old Mrs Casper, I could hardly credit her with such behaviour.

It had grown late by this time, and, as the store-room was very dimly lighted, I postponed the reading of the remaining diaries until the next day.

Alas, practically every one of them had suffered so badly from the incursions of the pests that I was unable to extract more than an occasional sentence or phrase from their contents. However, I did succeed in piecing together two more facts that were even more horrifying.

First, from the diary of 1937.

June 11. . . . on good authority . . . J. is keeping a woman . . . not a mile away . . .

Sept. 23. . . . outright . . . denied . . . obviously lying . . .

Sept. 30. . . . William acting very queerly again . . . way he looks at me . . .

Oct. 10. . . . quite true . . . tracked him . . .

Oct. 31. . . . sure that William knows . . . must act . . .

Dec. 15. . . . the old well . . . think I can . . .

The last few pages of this diary had become wedged together with the remainder of the batch to which it was tied, and it was impossible to distinguish more than a couple of letters here and there. But I called to mind, and checked up the next day in the public library's newspaper files of the February of the following year, the fate of John Jackson, chauffeur in the employ of Mrs Selina Casper of Camberly, who had fallen into an unused well in a field near his late employer's residence while in an intoxicated condition and had broken his neck.

Secondly, and perhaps the most shocking of all (although it is quite possible that I am mistaken in my conclusion, and, indeed, I sincerely hope I am), one entry, a single and unusually lengthy one, from the diary of 1939, one of the very few that had escaped mutilation, which contained no further entry after the date given:

Nov. 4. William still acting very queerly. His grandfather and his uncle both died insane. In 2 months' time he will be 21 and will inherit everything according to his father's will. I shall be little more than a pauper. How he hates me especially since . . .

As I say, I may be completely mistaken, but it is curious, to say the least, that William Arthur Morant, only son of Mrs Selina Casper and the late Nathan Morant, committed suicide while in an unsound state of mind on the second of January, 1940, two days before he would have attained his majority.

Thereafter the remaining diaries, some dozen of them of which only a very few had escaped complete defacement, contain little more than memoranda of accounts: of money spent, of money invested, or money received from investments and collection of rents.

The last one of the diaries was undamaged, and except for the aforesaid memoranda, contained two entries: one referring to my visit and containing the caustic comment: *they* (the diaries) *should knock some of the primness out of him*, a comment which I thought in rather poor taste; and the other, written the day before her death:

May 12. It should not be difficult. Let it be swift. The lorries pass by at 7.30. God . . .

Perhaps I may be allowed to finish the sentence for her: 'God forgive us all.'

The institution to which Mrs Casper bequeathed her small fortune is, I am glad to say, doing remarkably well. It will soon be one hundred pounds the richer.

To Meet Her Mother

'Who it is you think you shovin'? Like you think you own the whole bus . . . and nearly mash off all o' me toes to besides . . .'

Fitzwilkinson Cumberbatch did not deign to reply. Tightly wedged in between two of the fattest hucksters he had ever encountered, he tried to deflate himself as much as possible and to stare ahead as though unconscious of the speaker's rude remarks. And he was *not* pushing. It was not his fault that he had inadvertently trodden on the toes of one of the fat women when he was climbing into the bus. She had a large basket in her lap, and stepping over her had not been an easy matter.

God, how he loathed fat women! To him, they were the revolting opposites of all that constituted his ideal of femininity. He could never see a fat woman without being profoundly affected, nauseated almost.

He would have lighted a cigarette had he been able to move his arms without undue difficulty, but he thought better of it. The journey would soon be over.

And it was no use worrying about the creases in his new suit or the possible smell of fish that might accompany him when he got out. He would turn his thoughts to something else, something far more conducive to his peace of mind. He would let that swarm of pleasant fancies, growing increasingly more alluring during the past few weeks, and now leaving room for little else in his imagination, take over.

For Fitzwilkinson Cumberbatch was in love. And not merely in love, but consumed by the desire to take all possible steps to make the object of his affection, in the not too far distant future, his bride.

His bride! How inexpressibly lovely she was, his Sylphide! How precisely did the name evoke her image! A sylph, a sylph of Greek mythology, a creature of the air, graceful, delicate, glowing, altogether enchanting, a perfect example of the female form divine . . .

The huckster on his left spraddled her legs a bit wider to accommodate her basket and Fitzwilkinson was compelled to shrink a little further into his seat, but even this did not disturb the tenor of his reverie.

He had first met her at a party. He had been immediately attracted by her slim loveliness – she must have been about seventeen – but he had been much too shy to do more than offer her a sandwich. Then, a few days later, he had seen her on the beach. She had remembered him, had waved invitingly to him. They had bathed together. She was wearing a modest bikini, and his mind had been made up there and then. This girl would be his wife.

At the age of twenty-four, Fitzwilkinson Cumberbatch was well satisfied with his position as a clerk at a wholesale merchant's in the city. His employer thought very highly of him, and Fitzwilkinson did not doubt for a moment that any employer could have thought less. He was fully conscious of his worth. He had earned a raise in salary three times in as many years, and in another few months' time he would be able to own a car, a second-hand one perhaps but still something worthwhile – no more buses for him – and in another year most likely he would be able to afford marriage. He was careful with his money, avoided strong drink and bad companions, both male and female, and lived respectably and frugally with his mother, a small but dominant personality, who had reared him carefully and sent him to the best school she could afford. There he had done quite well, and had attained certificates in English Literature and Elementary Mathematics. The latter had stood him good stead in obtaining a job, and his study of the set books for the former had provided him with quite a store of the poems of Keats and Shelley.

Very often he would quote some of his favourite passages to Sylphide, modestly, almost as though they were his own.

For after the meeting on the beach, he had managed to meet her much more often. True, he had made no positive declaration of his love; had met her and her little sister occasionally at the cinema; had even travelled part of the way home with her on the bus; had conversed with her several times on the beach on Sunday mornings; had sent her a card on St Valentine's Day; but he had no doubt whatever that she would be only too pleased, in the course of time, to accept him as the man in her life, her husband-to-be. Why, had she not invited him, with the full knowledge and approval of her mother, to visit her at her home this very afternoon?

He wriggled ecstatically in his seat, and both hucksters glowered at him. But he took no notice of them.

I'm sure her mother must be a most discriminating woman, he thought. She certainly would not have consented to her daughter's inviting any and every young man of her acquaintance to her home. And he pictured her as Sylphide grown to maturity, beautiful, gracious, statuesque . . .

Sylphide, her little sister, Angela, and their mother, a widow, had but lately arrived from British Guiana. He had never met their mother – that was as yet a treat in store. She was a Mrs Robinson; but despite the surname, he was sure they were of Portuguese descent. The light brown complexion of the girls and their dark hair (raven locks, he liked to think of them) hinted at European ancestry. It would be a step up the social ladder for him when the marriage came off. Even the announcement of the engagement. And his mother had been most cooperative when he had told her of his attachment and of the family's social status. 'Always look for something higher than you, son,' she had affirmed.

The huckster whose toes he had trodden on scratched herself searchingly, vigorously, her arm jabbing him in his ribs.

He tried to edge away a little more to the right. He could not restrain the look of scorn with which he glanced disapprovingly at her.

'What happen to you now?' she queried. 'What you wrinklin' up your nose for?' And, furnishing an answer to her unacknowledged question, 'If you smell something nasty, mus' be your own top lip.'

This was too much. People sitting near him had begun to titter.

The bus had stopped. Sylphide's house was only a couple of hundred yards further on. So he rose, deliberately stepped on the huckster's canvas-covered toes, and hopped out awkwardly, followed by a stream of abuse and the now unchecked guffaws of those of the passengers who had witnessed the incident.

Trying to rid himself of every semblance of contact with those two horrible creatures, he flicked off imaginary specks of contamination from his smart outfit, and wished that somehow all fat women could be boiled down, the more painfully the better, to respectable size. 'Damn monsters,' he said to himself as the bus groaned past him, belching out its fumes and the last echoes of its occupants' remarks.

He lit a cigarette and glanced at his wrist watch. Seven minutes past four. Sylphide had invited him to come at half-past. He would be in good time.

He glanced around him approvingly as he strolled along. Yes, a most desirable district. All the houses, neat and clean and showing obvious signs of being lived in by people of some consequence. Flowers bloomed in the front gardens, curtains flapped from most of the windows, a canary chirped from a cage on one of the open verandahs, and a radio barked out, but very discreetly, the chorus of a popular song.

He walked on.

One of the tidiest and trimmest of the stone bungalows bore the inscription, 'The Cedars'. What a pretty name, he thought, ignoring the fact that it was completely overshadowed by a large tamarind tree and nothing else. How appropriate that his Sylphide should live in a house that bore such a romantic name!

He went up the short flight of steps. The door was closed. He rapped loudly. Twice.

The door was opened by a neat-looking maid wearing a blue denim dress and newly-ironed cap and apron.

'Good afternoon,' he said. 'I am Mr Fitzwilkinson Cumberbatch. I think your mistress and Miss Sylphide are expecting me.'

The maid grinned at him. 'Hey, it is you already? Miss Sylphie jus' step out, down the road for a few minutes, but she tell me was to tell you when you come she soon comin' back. And the mistress dressin'. She say if it is you, please to come in and have a seat.'

'Thank you.'

'And she tell me was to open up the winders so as you could get some fresh air.'

Thanking her again, Fitzwilkinson followed her, and, while she opened the two windows looking out on to the street, took stock of his surroundings.

He was most pleased by what he saw. The large settee, the chairs – easy chairs and straight-backed chairs, the rug patterned with gigantic pink roses, the little mahogany tables, one of them covered with magazines, the small piano in the corner, the vases of flowers, the expensive-looking television set, the standard lamps, the colourful pictures that adorned the walls . . . everything bore unmistakable signs of . . . of quality . . . of money.

He was exceedingly pleased. Perhaps he too would be able some day to furnish his home like this . . . perhaps an even larger piano, a rather more expensive television set . . .

'I goin' call Miss Sylphie now,' the maid announced, having finished her task. And she went out through the front door.

Fitzwilkinson chose the most comfortable-looking of the easy chairs beside the table with the magazines. Four or five minutes passed. It was almost half-past four.

He glanced at one or two of the magazines, but *Woman* and *Woman This*, and *Woman's That* were not to his taste. But beside them lay a photograph album. It looked as though it had seen better days.

This might be interesting, he thought. He picked it up and turned the pages eagerly.

But he was disappointed. Unknown faces stared back at him. Unknown houses, unknown lawns, unknown scenes. It was obvious that all the photos had been taken some time ago and before the family had come to Barbados. Still, there might have been a picture of Sylphide as a little girl, as a baby perhaps . . . how irritating . . .

He had almost reached the last page and was about to close the album, when a loose photograph slipped out and fluttered to the carpet at his feet.

He stooped and picked it up.

He gazed at it entranced.

Whoever had taken that picture had certainly known his job. Here was the living image of his dreams, his Sylphide, clad in some gauzy creation, a fancy-costume of some sort . . . fairy-like, ethereal . . . her dark eyes shining, her lips smiling, smiling so tenderly, so ravishingly . . . as though to meet his enthralled regard.

'Sylphide, my Sylph, my beloved!' he whispered, and was about to raise this miracle of the photographer's art to his lips, when he noticed a few specks of dust on it.

He sighed deeply instead.

After a few moments he looked through the album again quickly to see where it had come from, but all the spaces enclosed by the photo-mounts were filled. Perhaps it had just been pushed in, casually – perhaps whoever had put it there had forgotten all about it.

He glanced around him cautiously. Could he possibly – steal it?

He hesitated.

And before he could quite make up his mind to transfer it to his pocket, he was aware that he was no longer alone.

Someone had entered the room noiselessly. Someone was standing at its far corner and looking at him intently.

Whether the expression on the person's face was kindly disposed or not, he was in no condition to observe; for the person, a lady, who was now advancing to meet him, waddling across the intervening space of carpet with outstretched hand, and who he realised must be Sylphide's mother, was, without exception, the fattest woman he had ever laid eyes on. All the corpulent females who from time to time had left their gross impressions on the screen of his memory were mere wisps when compared with the agglomeration of flesh that now confronted him.

How he managed to rise and allow his hand to be engulfed in the tepid flabbiness of the lady's he had no idea.

Nor had he any idea of what she was saying as she chattered on during the first few moments after her greeting. He was only conscious of a mounting sensation of weakness, of complete mental haziness, as though his whole world was collapsing around him.

Eventually his mind cleared sufficiently for him to grasp the import of her words.

'. . . had to go on a little message for me . . . just a few houses down the road . . . I can't move around quite as quickly as she can . . .' And she chuckled hoarsely, quivering all over like some preposterous blob of blancmange.

Fitzwilkinson could only smile weakly in reply. His tongue was drained dry of words.

'Sylphie has told me so much about you . . .' she went on.

Could he possibly endure a mother-in-law such as this? he wondered. Can I go on seeing her, talking to her, perhaps even having to live in the same house with her some day? Was this too big a price to pay for Sylphide?

The voice continued: ' . . . such a nice boy, she tells me, not like most of these rough young fellows one is so apt to meet almost anywhere nowadays, it seems . . .'

Perhaps, perhaps, he *could* make the sacrifice.

And a thought struck him: People as fat as this don't live long. He remembered how suddenly Mrs Cullup, who used to live next door, had gone off.

He plucked up courage and smiled again, a little less wanly. And he then realised she was looking at the photograph he was still holding in his hand.

It was time for him to say something, after all. He moistened his lips and discovered that he could speak.

'What a lovely photo of your daughter, Mrs Robinson,' he exclaimed, handing it to her. 'While I was waiting, I was looking through your album and I found this.'

Mrs Robinson looked at the photograph and smiled back at him.

'How beautiful Sylphide is!' he rattled on, now that he was no longer afraid of his voice failing him. 'And how very charming she looks in that old-fashioned costume!'

Mrs Robinson's response to these remarks was astonishing in the extreme. She began to laugh. To chuckle at first, shaking all over, even more disgustingly than before. Then to laugh, to cackle, louder and louder.

He could only stare.

And then, when she had regained her breath and had mopped her face:

'But, young man, that is *me*, eh? That is a picture of me taken when I was just Sylphie's age. You don't see the resemblance *now*, eh?'

And again spasms of *uncontrollable* laughter shook her entire frame.

When, a few moments later, Sylphide arrived, Fitzwilkinson Cumberbatch had disappeared.

A Day at the Races

Everybody went to the Races. For days they had been the unceasing topic of conversation at school. Completely ignorant of the merits of the various horses, Mark had to keep a discreet silence and listen to Sammy and Henry and Dudley who spoke with authority, especially to Henry, whose father knew one of the trainers personally.

Every day there would be animated discussions on the current form of the two horses, Jack-in-the-Box and Razor, which, for the past couple of years, had contended for the prize in the big race. Razor was a Barbadian horse ridden by a Barbadian jockey; Jack-in-the-Box was from Trinidad with an Englishman up, and Mark, though he felt that from patriotic considerations alone Razor should be the better horse, realised that this was hardly sufficient reason for him to enter the debate. So he was forced to maintain a moody silence, wishing with all his heart that he might witness the struggle himself.

The idea took root, grew. It would be very difficult, he knew. Had his father and mother been on the island, he might have persuaded them to take him to the races; but they were on holiday in Demerara, and he felt it would be hopeless to persuade the Aunts, with whom he was staying at Graham Lodge, to do so. Even though he was now nine years old, they would never consent to his going alone. Not even with Joe. Joe was the yard-boy who had been in their employ for as long as he could remember. But he had tried.

'Go to the races?' Aunt Jane had repeated. 'Most certainly not.'

'But why?'

'Don't be silly, child. Do you think we'd allow you to go up there in all that confusion?'

And Aunt Judy had chimed in: 'What's that? Races? Among all those ragamuffins! Nonsense.'

'But if Joe took me . . .'

But Aunt Jane had only snorted and walked off, and Aunt Judy had lectured him on the impropriety of his suggestion.

But he had made up his mind. He would go. He could not return to school after the meeting and stand by listening to what had happened – like Clara and Maude and the other girls.

One morning he had seen Razor passing by in charge of a groom. Joe had pointed him out to him. So he felt entitled to join in the conversation that day, at least. And Sammy, the head boy, had asked, 'Which stand you going in?' And Mark had explained that he didn't think he'd be going, since his aunts wouldn't let him, and Sammy had laughed and said, 'I'd like to see aunts or uncles trying to stop me. What are you . . . a baby or what?' And Mark had swallowed the insult and gone home that afternoon more than ever determined that he'd show them all he could take care of himself.

It was the eve of the meeting. The Aunts had reluctantly consented to Joe's taking him for a walk around the Savannah, so that, at least, he might catch a glimpse of the preparations. Usually, only soldiers were to be seen, some in red coats on parade, others enjoying a game of football; but this afternoon everything was different, exciting. Lots of civilians were strolling around. The grandstand with a new coat of whitewash immediately caught his eye. And there were three other stands, temporary constructions of rough, sweet-smelling pine. And several strange little ones on wheels, which he discovered to be large plantation carts, almost inconceivably transformed by means of tarpaulins and steps into their present entrancing appearance. And more and more people were congregating, many of them obviously country-folk, and, what was altogether remarkable, was the fact that some of them, dressed in their Sunday-best, were carrying their footwear slung over their shoulders.

'Them does come from the country,' Joe explained, 'and, as them ain't 'custom to shoes, them does walk down barefoot so as not to let the shoes bite them.'

'And when do they put them on?'

'When they dress for the races tomorrow.'

But Mark couldn't understand. 'But why don't they dress and come down tomorrow?'

'Them come already. You see, they lives so far, they does come down the evenin' before and sleep 'pon the spot so as to be nice and fresh.'

'How you mean – sleep on the spot?'

'Right here, na? Sleep wherever they can. Most o' them will mek friends with the watchman and sleep onderneat' the stands.'

The enthusiasm of these poor country-folk which led them to brave the discomfort of new shoes and the perils of the night served to strengthen Mark's resolve only the more. But he would tell no one. Not even Joe.

They lingered for a while, Mark secretly hoping that he might see some of them preparing to go to bed, until Joe reminded him that it would soon be dark, and that he wanted to see the wooden horses.

At every meeting a merry-go-round would be set up in an open space adjoining the Garrison, and through his bedroom window for the last few nights Mark had heard the continuous beat of drums and the piercing notes of the fife that speeded the wooden horses on their never-ending journey.

On leaving the Garrison Savannah, they passed through what appeared to be somebody's backyard and arrived at the merry-go-round. It was quite inactive now; the fun would not begin until after dark. The canvas roof was grimy and tattered; a ragged Union Jack flew jauntily above. From the rim of the circular roof there hung in pairs, by means of rusty iron rods, blocks of wood which Mark realised were supposed to represent the horses. They dangled forlornly, swaying ever so slightly in the evening breeze, and as he drew nearer, he was shocked to see that they had been painted in such a way as to destroy the last illusion of reality: some were blue, some green, and others daubed with large yellow spots. But from age and use they had all become drab and worn; in some places the plain wood showed through.

'Let's go home now, Joe,' Mark said. A sort of impersonal compassion for these absurd travesties overwhelmed him: to obtain further contact with them would have been as impossible as to make fun of old Miss Martha, toothless and blind, who occupied a room at Graham Lodge with the Aunts.

'Early to bed, early to rise' was the Aunts' motto, and by eight o'clock Mark blew out the light in the attic and made ready for sleep. But sleep would not come. The incessant drumming that accompanied the whirl of the wooden horses, the shrill blasts of the fife, and the laughter and shrieks of the riders borne on the breeze mocked his desire. When he did drop off, he slept restlessly: the blunt, sightless faces of the wooden horses haunted his dreams. He rode them now, down long darkened lanes that merged fantastically into the drawing room of Graham Lodge and the schoolroom of the Driscolls', with Sammy and the other boys close behind him, laughing at him. 'He can't go out by himself, you know . . . Baby Mark . . . Baby Mark . . .'

He woke late. There was no school on race days. The morning yawned emptily. How could he fill up the time until one o'clock? And, far more important, how could he escape without being noticed? He laid his plans most carefully. No one must have the remotest suspicion of his intention. He helped Aunt Jane in the garden, dusted Aunt Judy's books for her, read a chapter of the Bible for old Miss Martha.

He didn't dare put on his best suit at lunch time. His school clothes would have to do. And he had to manufacture some excuse for appearing at lunch with his shoes on. 'Going to pick some cherries presently. Lots of burrs in the grasspiece.'

At last lunch was over. The household dozed. Joe had gone home and wouldn't be back until four. He strolled out casually in the direction of the cherry tree. From there he could make a better escape through the tenantry, which blocked the view of anyone from the house, until he reached the street. But this manoeuvre had taken a little time. He reckoned it must be well past two o'clock by now. But it was only a few minutes' walk to the Savannah.

He emerged from the tenantry alley into the street. Well, he wouldn't be the only late-comer. He joined a long stream of people hurrying, some actually running, on their way to the course. He had to walk warily, keep to the gutter almost, for there were not only people – buggies, bicycles, horse-drawn cabs and buses, and donkey-carts were all proceeding in the same direction, and with a blare of whistles, four mule-drawn tram-cars, all packed to capacity, rolled by.

As the stream turned up Bush Hill, it was brought to a temporary halt. Two cabs had somehow got their wheels interlocked, and consequently no fewer than three policemen had relinquished their posts to hurry to the spot, thereby leaving the traffic to become just as hopelessly entangled.

Mark, securely wedged in between a growing and impatient crowd, was enjoying himself thoroughly. He was wondering what the Aunts would have said, had they been present, to have heard the ceaseless stream of profanity which the two cab-drivers were dispensing to each other, to the policemen, and to the world at large. And the driver of an old ramshackle horse-bus, acutely conscious of the waste of valuable time, was leaning back in his seat in despair, his reins dangling dejectedly, and moaning at intervals through his broken, discoloured teeth, 'Oh hell . . . oh bloody hell . . .'

And then, almost miraculously the two cabs became disentangled, and the waiting crowd, suddenly released from their enforced halt, surged forward, rushing up the hill helter-skelter, bearing Mark along with them.

A terrific noise of shouting and cheering informed him that a race was now in progress. The noise, however, was insufficient to drown the shrill cries of 'Race bills, race bills!' from the many urchins along the roadside, waving wads of gaudy pink and blue and yellow paper which they thrust into the faces of the passers-by.

Before he could reach the top of the hill, the shouting and cheering had subsided, and a man, his shirt almost torn from his sweaty chest, came pushing his way through the crowd. 'Jack-in-the-Box win!' he shouted as though it was his duty to spread the news. 'Jack-in-the-Box win!' Ah well, he'd missed the race and Razor hadn't won; but this wasn't the big race, Mark consoled himself.

He was glad when he was able to break away from the crowd and stop for a few moments under one of the evergreens which bordered the Savannah. He looked about him. People, people everywhere. They were all now trickling back from the positions they had taken in order to witness the race, and soon he found himself in the midst of a chattering, gesticulating gathering, which proceeded to give its impressions, criticisms and illustrative comments on what it had just seen. As its ardour abated, it dispersed to buy refreshments from the many vendors seated near by: cakes, fruit, black pudding and souse, and enormous jars of ginger beer, lemonade and mauby.

From scraps of conversation, Mark gathered that although Razor had lost this race, he was 'holding back' for the important one later in the afternoon. And he remembered that Henry had predicted just such a thing, and he wondered where he and Sammy and Dudley were at this moment. He looked around vainly for signs of any of his schoolmates. Well, he'd come on his own, so he'd have to fend for himself. The first thing to do would be to find some position from which he could view the next race. He wormed his way through the crowd. He could glimpse the white-washed fence which bordered the course, and he determined to get there somehow. Luck was with him, for at that moment, two men had passed from argument to blows, and, the crowd having parted to give them elbowroom, he seized the opportunity and managed to get fairly close to his goal.

A long-legged, brownskinned man with an enormous reddish moustache, seeing his efforts, made room for him, and Mark, smiling acknowledgement of his kindness, was soon standing beside him, his chin resting on the rail of the fence.

'See all right?' asked the man, bending forward.

'Yes, thank you,' he replied.

The man bent forward again until his moustache almost touched Mark's nose. 'You rather small to be out, all by yourself,' he said in a kindly voice – but just a bit too inquisitively, Mark thought.

And a woman, standing on the other side joined in: 'Yo' mammy let you come up here by you one?'

Mark grunted a non-committal reply.

'All's right, boysie, I ain't nothin' to do with you. But best be careful.' And, with this admonition, she ceased from further enquiry and began to sing a hymn very loudly.

Left thus to himself, Mark took note of his surroundings. On the opposite side of the course, there was a long row of carriages which extended almost to the paddock. The horses had all been removed from the shafts, the carriage-hoods were let down, and seated in these makeshift stands, numbers of people, ladies chiefly, were eating and chatting merrily. Under the carriages, their heads projecting at the most unexpected places, could be seen dozens of urchins who had thus secured the shelter of a safe but cramped lookout. Beyond the carriages, the crowd swarmed denser than ever. Above their heads, Mark could see a man on stilts dancing. Here and there in little clumps of twos and threes he could distinguish khaki-clad soldiers. Craning his neck over the low fence, he could also see some of the quaint stands that had so intrigued him on the previous evening.

Somewhere the military band was playing. A bell rang sharply. People began to flock back to the rails. And now the wind began to stir up all sorts of odd bits of paper and other litter, and a straw hat pursued by its owner came rolling down the straight run. There was loud laughter and comment from the crowd: 'Don't let she beat you, son' . . . 'Use yo' whip, boy' . . . until the wayward hat stopped so suddenly that its owner plunged his foot through the crown. As he made no attempt to leave the course, but continued to gaze sorrowfully at his ruined hat, a policeman darted out and led him off hurriedly; not a moment too soon, as the first of the horses came cantering down the track.

It passed very close to where Mark was standing. The little jockey reminded him of a toy monkey on a stick, seeming barely able to restrain its whimsical capers. How pretty it was!

Another race was about to begin.

As the first horse passed by, Mark could hardly restrain his excitement.

'What horse is that?' he asked the tall man with the moustache.

'That's Julie. And she's a mare.'

'Look at another one!' exclaimed Mark.

Another, and another, and another, and yet another. Five in all. Beautiful, graceful things. How kittenish they were! Never quiet for a moment. They passed by daintily, the last one at a slow mincing walk, with rearing, nervous head. A beauty it was.

Darkish, with a bright splash of white on its forehead. Its jockey wore a silvery coat. 'Silver Star, Silver Star!' yelled the crowd

'I like that one,' Mark said.

'You ain't far wrong, sonny. Watch him eat up the course.'

At this remark, another man, standing next to Mark's tall friend and wearing a large brass tiepin in the form of a horse's head, interposed: 'Does I onderstand you to remark that the favour of your judgement is given to the horse, Silver Star?'

'Ondoubtedly,' said the tall man.

'Then permit me to contract a small bet with you. I begs to tek you on at evens that he do not win this race.'

Whereupon the tall man retorted 'Done', and taking out a large wallet, 'I'll back Silver Star for ten bob.'

'Mek it a dollar,' said the man with the tiepin, 'and I'll be pleased to coincide.'

'Ah, come on,' said the tall man. 'A dollar scarce worthwhile winning.'

'Peradventure I isn't as rolling in wealth as you, but lewwe call it a deal at five bob.'

'Okay. Who holds the bet? . . . Ah, look here, here's a young gentleman' (indicating Mark) 'who'll be pleased to do so.'

The man with the tiepin stretched out two half-crowns to Mark. 'Is you willing to serve in that capacity?'

'Do what?' asked Mark.

'Hold the bets. We each gives you five shillin's, and when the race is over, you hands the total amount to the one who is victorious.'

Visions of the Aunts' faces, set in frowns of disapproval, flashed across Mark's conscience. Betting! ! ! What should he do?

'You don't mind, little feller?' asked the tall man persuasively.

Mark received the money from the two men after some hesitation. Betting, gambling, drinking . . . these things were all sinful, weren't they? But the tall man had been so nice to him that he felt it would be ungracious of him to refuse.

With an added air of interest, he watched the horses canter past to the starting-place which was quite out of sight from his viewpoint. However, the tall man, observing Mark's futile efforts to catch a glimpse of what was taking place, caught him up suddenly without warning, and set him right on top of the fence, placing an arm securely around his waist.

From his new position, Mark could see the stands. They were packed with people, most of whom were standing and gazing in the direction where the horses had lined up for the start. He could see over the heads of the crowd where it clustered thickest, the bright coats of the jockeys moving this way and that as their restless mounts pranced and side-stepped. There was a confused babbling murmur. A breeze had sprung up and bits of paper and straw whirled and fluttered down the course. And then the babble swelled to a roar . . . 'Off, off!'

Away went three of the coloured coats. They seemed to be floating over the heads of the crowd.

And then another shout: 'False start!' A shout caught and re-echoed by everyone around him. One of the coats hadn't budged – the green one.

'That's Julie,' observed Mark's protector. 'Every meetin' she does get on with that damn foolishness.'

Back went the coloured coats. Again the line-up. Again the shout OFF OFF! Again the cry FALSE START. And a third time the same thing happened.

'I beg you to observe where Silver Star gone this time,' chuckled the man with the brass tiepin. 'I tell you she can't win this race. She exhausting her energeticalness to too great a extension.'

The tall man growled a non-committal answer to this observation. There seemed some sense in what Tiepin was saying, though, for Mark noticed that the silver coat was quite a good distance from the starting-point. He watched it return, slowly. And then he saw them all dart off, silver coat, after an appreciable pause, in the rear.

OFF OFF OFF . . . a swelling thunderous roar. A bell rang loudly. Off! Now that they had emerged from the crowd, Mark could see them clearly. The green coat, closely followed by two others, was far ahead. 'Julie, Julie!' roared the crowd. Silver coat was away behind.

Mark felt the arm encircling him trembling. He looked round at the tall man apprehensively. He seemed to have gone to pieces.

Even his moustache drooped sadly. But Tiepin was dancing with delight.

The horses were right over on the opposite side of the Savannah now. They looked no bigger than rats. How slowly they seemed to move! The space between the green coat and the others widened. The grip around Mark's waist tightened. A few drops of rain fell on Mark's face. He looked up. The sky had suddenly become overcast. The wind freshened. And then – suddenly – like another rush of wind, the roaring of the crowd increased in volume. 'Silver Star, Silver Star!' And Mark saw the silver coat draw closer and closer to those in front. The arm around his waist began to squeeze him tighter and tighter. Just as the horses turned to enter the straight run they were temporarily out of sight. The little boys under the carriages darted out right on to the course, and then just as swiftly returned. The horses had entered the straight. Mark could hear the music of their hooves. Beautiful! Then they came into view. Who was in front? Mark craned forward. Thud, thud, thud, beat the hooves. Chests straining, slim forelegs thrusting forward, rhythmically, powerfully.

And, as they swept past, in a brief photographic moment, he saw Silver Star draw abreast of the leading horses, leave them behind as though they were stationary, and take the lead as they flashed along to the finish amid a tornado of howling, cheering noises. And with a start Mark realised that he had been shouting too. The tall man, swinging him abruptly to the ground, removed his hat and waved it aloft.

'Boy, what for a race you call that, na?'

Tiepin, collapsed on the rail, would vouchsafe no answer.

'Drop the coppers in here, sonny. That was a race!'

Mark did as he was bid.

The tall man cocked an eye upwards. 'Hey, like we going get some rain.'

It was drizzling steadily now, and the sky was leaden. People were beginning to move away.

'We better get a shelter, sonny. Come.'

Clasping the hand of the tall man who walked very rapidly on his stork-like legs, Mark was forced to break into a trot. He had no idea where his guide was leading him, but he could hear the sound of the oncoming rain now, close at hand. They had reached the main road that encircled the Savannah.

'I tryin' to get onder one of the stands,' the man shouted above the din. Mark nodded and increased his pace.

And at that moment a cry of alarm was raised. A mounted policeman's horse, excited by the increasing tumult, had got out of control, and was bearing down directly upon them. And the rain was now down in full force. As the tall man stepped aside to avoid the oncoming animal, he slipped, relinquished his hold on Mark's hand, and disappeared from the latter's sight as magically as though he had never existed. Mark himself was swept away in the opposite direction by the crowd as the frightened horse galloped past, and before he could recover from the shock of all that had happened, he found himself in front of a marquee on a grass plot on the opposite side of the road. And then one of the canvas flaps blew open, and, before he knew what was happening, he received a sudden push from behind, and plunged blindly forward into the crowded interior. A matronly woman, whom he had thus inadvertently collided with, smiled at him and drew him away from the flapping canvas.

'Come in out o' the rain, darlin',' she said. 'You wet enough already.'

Mark thanked her and looked around him.

He could see but very little from where he stood, since the interior of the tent was packed with all sorts of people who had come in to shelter. They were all talking and jabbering away, most of them dripping wet. At the far end of the marquee there was a bar of some sort. Mark could see above the heads of the crowd many rows of bottles of liquor, and there were loud shouts from those who had clustered around calling for drinks. The noise was deafening. He stood there, wedged in between the woman who had assisted him, and three nut-sellers. He had a few pennies in his pocket, so he thought he might as well pass the time shelling and eating some nuts. The rain played an unceasing tattoo on the roof and sides of the marquee. How long would it continue? More and more people pushed their way in. For the first time he wished he was back home at Graham Lodge. It was so snug and cosy there when it rained like this. And the Aunts, how distressed they must be! Aunt Jane wouldn't be able to find any pleasure in her reading of yesterday's newspaper, and Aunt Judy's crochet would be completely disregarded. What were they doing? He hoped they wouldn't be crying . . .

After what seemed like hours the downpour slackened to a steady drizzle and a feeble long-drawn shout announced that another race was about to begin. People began to leave the tent but Mark decided he would wait until the rain stopped altogether: it was more comfortable now. Besides, this wasn't the big race, the one he had come to see.

And then the rain came down again, and again the marquee was filled to overflowing. The minutes dragged by. And then, amid the raucous hubbub and confusion, one of the nut-sellers began to sing:

> Before the hills in order stood
> Or earth received its frame . . .

and soon others caught up the words of the hymn, and in a short while it might have been a revivalist meeting in progress.

And then, suddenly, the rain stopped. The sky was blue. The sun was shining.

In a few moments, with the exception of the barman and his attendants, the marquee was empty.

What should he do now? Go home? But then he'd miss the race he'd come to see. His clothes were almost soaked through and his shoes were covered with mud. How would he find his way back to the fence? Would he be lucky enough to find the tall man? Jumping over the swollen gutter, he picked his way across the miry road, and narrowly escaped bumping into a barefooted young man carrying an open umbrella. Mark glanced back at the young man. Those legs with the uprolled trousers looked startlingly familiar.

'Joe!' Mark shouted as he rushed after him.

Joe turned so swiftly that he almost skidded on the slushy road. 'Masta Mark!'

'The Aunts sent you?'

'But Masta Mark, how you could go and do a thing like this?'

Mark laughed. He could afford to laugh now. 'They wouldn't let me come. But how did they know I was here at the races?'

'Yo' Aunt Jane send me to ax 'bout the place if anybody seen you, and old Miss Tull in the tenantry tell me she see you turn the corner 'bout two o'clock and head for the Savannah.'

Mark laughed again. 'I can take care of myself, you know.'

'And you wet; you wet wet wet.'

'Not much. I sheltered in there.' And he pointed to the rain-sodden marquee opposite.

'Well, come. Lewwe go back. Your Aunt Judy in a state.'

'How?'

'She ain't cryin' and that's all. Come lewwe go.'

But Mark stood firm. 'Listen, Joe. I want to see the next race, the big one. I haven't seen Razor and Jack-in-the-Box yet, and they're going to run now. A man told me so.'

'I isn't waitin', Masta Mark.'

'And I ain't going, see?'

'But you must.'

'Now look here, Joe. They're soon going to run the race. Just wait till then, and I'll come. True, true.'

Joe hesitated. He had wanted to see the race himself.

'If I lets you stay till then, you'll come? Promise?'

'Promise. Come let's get a good place. I know where to go,' said Mark, making off.

But Joe stopped him. 'You come with me. I knows a better.' And proceeded to lead him back up the road over which the wooden stands towered.

'Where you going, Joe?'

But Joe only winked. At the base of a flight of steps leading up to one of the stands Joe halted and looked up to where a short elderly man was standing guard. He waved at him and the man waved back. Joe led Mark up the steps. He then shook hands with the man and entered into a hurried whispered conversation with him. The man looked up, shouted something to another man on the platform above them, and Joe and Mark, climbing another flight of steps, found themselves standing on a bench, behind a number of little stalls in which rows of well-dressed ladies, gentlemen and children were gazing out on the entire course spread out before them.

'How you manage, Joe?' Mark whispered.

'Shhhh. That man I speak to in charge o' the stand married to my mother half-sister. Shhh.'

The bell rang. The horses were out. Together, in relative comfort, Mark and Joe watched them line up, six of them, and dart away without a single false start. Razor and Jack-in-the-Box soon left the others far behind, and, as they swept up the straight, mud flying from their pounding hooves, Razor flashed past his rival and finished first by almost a length.

'Come now, Masta Mark,' urged Joe. 'It gettin' on to half-past four, and the rain buildin' again. Come!'

So down the muddy stairs, a word of thanks to Joe's relative, and quickly, very quickly, back to Graham Lodge.

The Aunts met them at the doorway. Then such a fuss ensued, such questioning, such clapping of his clothing to determine whether or not he would catch his death of cold (for one of the Aunts' brothers had, many years ago, contracted pneumonia after a similar experience), that Mark found it difficult to discover whether he was being scolded for his disobedience or congratulated on his safe return.

That evening, lying on the drawing-room rug, and listening to the steady drip of the rain which had been falling continuously since his return, Mark felt very happy. Aunt Judy had told him, her soft eyes full of tears, how terribly his disobedience had affected her, and he had told her how sorry he was to have frightened her so, but inwardly he could not feel any regret for what he had done. As the thronging events of the day, thick as a swarm of bees, recurred to his mind, he sat upright to recount his adventures all over again for the fourth or fifth time. He felt that Aunt Judy had forgiven him, but he wasn't so sure of Aunt Jane.

'And he put his arm around me and held me and told me the names of all the horses . . .'

'And did you ask him his name?' queried Aunt Judy.

'No. But he was very nice. And he had a reddish moustache and he kept his arm around me all the time . . .'

'There now,' said Aunt Judy, 'see how God sent someone to protect you.'

'But, Aunt Judy, I don't think God sent him.' Mark lowered his voice. 'You see, he was . . . he was *betting*.'

From the depths of her easy-chair, Aunt Jane emitted one of those throaty guffaws that Mark so loved to hear. He realised, then, that she too had forgiven him.

'I had a l-l-lovely day.'

The Aunts looked at each other. Aunt Jane shook a warning finger.

'We don't intend punishing you, Mark, but please remember: don't ever do a thing like that again. Don't think only of yourself; remember that we love you, dear, and the thought of you all alone on that race course . . .'

Mark embraced the Aunts fervently. They were really nice.

And, next day, Mark discovered that with the exception of Henry, he had been the only boy to go to the races. Dudley had had to attend his grandmother's funeral, Arthur had preferred to join some friends of his in a game of backyard cricket, and Sammy, twelve-year-old Sammy, this was the cream of it – Sammy's mother had not allowed him to go by himself!

That day everyone crowded around Henry and Mark. He could now speak with authority.

Afterword

When Frank Collymore began editing *Bim* in the 1940s, there did not yet exist a substantial body of distinctly West Indian literature. This emerged in the decades which followed, thanks in part to Collymore's strenuous efforts to ensure the survival of *Bim* and hence provide a soil for a growing West Indian literature.

Born in the parish of St Michael, Barbados, in 1893, Frank Collymore had a long and distinguished career. As a teacher at Barbados's famous Combermere, where he himself had been a student, he had a profound influence on the development of several notable West Indians – George Lamming, Austin Clarke and the island's future Prime Minister, Errol Barrow. He was also a man of letters, an imaginative painter, and reputed to be one of Barbados's finest actors. Although his poetry has been anthologied and collected – he published three volumes – his eighteen short stories, all published in *Bim* between 1942 and 1971,[1] have gone largely unnoticed. This is unfortunate since many of them are pieces of fine quality, and merit a place in any collection of first-rate West Indian short fiction.

With one or two exceptions, all of Collymore's short stories have West Indian characters and settings. It must be said, however, that the settings and characters are not as palpably West Indian as were those of his predecessors, C. L. R. James and Alfred Mendes. This may have been deliberate, since Collymore and his colleagues did not wish *Bim*, in its infancy at any rate, to pursue 'a policy of exclusive West Indianness'.[2] Collymore's themes, consequently, are not uniquely West Indian: at least six of his stories explore the dark underside of human beings; several examine disturbing, and certainly profound, issues such as alienation and loneliness.

Collymore was not a pointedly political writer, but he did not eschew socio-political issues. His fondness for socio-political satire is evident in 'RSVP to Mrs Bush-Hall' (1962). Mrs Bush-Hall – the hyphenated name points to her smug pretentiousness – has risen from prostitution and promiscuity to the status of shallow socialite for whom good form and *noblesse oblige* are the indispensable qualities of a sham respectability. She sees fulfilment for her equally shallow daughter Pyrlene in marriage to Lucas, a mediocre poet. An English expatriate, Lucas thrives in colonial Barbados and is considered an eminently suitable catch. Here is Mrs Bush-Hall barely able to contain her exhilaration at her daughter's engagement:

> It was to be the most wonderful party ever. Something that would be talked about for many a long day, something that would take up at least a column in *Carib*, something that would make her, Maude Bush-Hall, the most envied of mothers in Barbados. For at the party there would be the announcement of her daughter's engagement – not to a mere civil service clerk . . . but, if you please, to a member of the British Aristocracy who was, incidentally, a literary celebrity . . .

In the obtuse, inferiority-ridden, colonial society Collymore depicts, Lucas's Englishness is sufficient guarantee of his integrity and worth. Lucas, however, is a thief and con-man. He robs mother, jilts daughter, and flees Barbados while the engagement party is in progress. Yet, Mrs Bush-Hall can nonetheless still admire Lucas's audacity. She saves face by making up a story which not only explains away Lucas's sudden departure, but more importantly is also a defence of the Old Country. Her face-saving is, after all, a matter of *noblesse oblige*.

Two of Collymore's stories, 'Shadows' (1942) and 'Rewards and Chrysanthemums' (1961), the first published at the start of his career under the pseudonym of Francis Appleton, the second towards the mid-point, show his fascination with the dark underside of the human mind and his ability to create atmosphere and tone with sparse yet stylish prose. In 'Shadows' Poe's influence, especially 'The Fall of the House of Usher', is noticeable. Collymore's narrator shares Usher's abnormal seclusion, loneliness and hypersensitivity. The house, whose sinister 'shadows' seem to threaten his very being, resembles a sentient creature, which is one of the features of Usher's house; and the room where he was born is particularly forbidding:

> . . . I was aware of the strangeness of that particular room . . . In its gloomy recesses lay thick shadows which invaded me day by day, but at night . . . the shadows thronged triumphant, whispering to me strange secrets, obscure and fleeting as my troubled dreams . . . The very soul of my room, I sometimes think, must have entered mine as the years rolled on, and subdued me to its vast, impersonal force which awaited but the allotted moment to crush me utterly.

Usher is convinced that the house and its ghastly environs have moulded the destinies of his family and turned him into a morbid and doomed creature. So also the reclusive narrator of 'Shadows', who speaks of his house 'with the unforgotten lives of past generations of our family lying thick about it'. But 'Shadows' ought not to be dismissed as mere imitation of Poe: the tone and language bear Collymore's terse signature, which does not have the earlier writer's brilliant flourishes. The events may not have actually taken place, and herein lies the real terror of the story: the recluse's growing realisation that he is losing his mind. His withdrawal from the society of men and women into the recesses of his own disturbed soul predisposes him to mental collapse. He is, furthermore, painfully aware of the fragility of the human mind, how easily it can be distorted, how easily it can snap. This is an additional source of terror. Read this way, the 'shadows' haunting him are the embodiment of those undefined but actual forces destroying his mind. If, on the other hand, the bizarre events did indeed take place, then it may be said that he pays for the crime of deliberately trying to possess another person, the unfortunate wife whose 'delicate and perfumed body . . . [he] had purchased in the social mart'. Having denied his wife her personhood, he in turn is about to fall into the abyss of mindlessness.

'Rewards and Chrysanthemums' is a remarkably controlled

examination of the fragile psyches of two Barbadian sisters, Maud and Joan, who are now living together after a separation of some twenty years in what may perhaps be described as anguished middle age. Joan, who has led an 'unconventional' life in America, is now drawn, irreversibly it would appear, into Maud's 'circumscribed range of conventionality' and morbid sensibilities. The narrative tone, which is sustained throughout the story by Collymore's moving yet undemonstrative style, is sombre, sympathetic and understated. There is no superfluous material in this fine story. The reader's focus on the sisters' tense, yet occasionally gentle, relationship never relaxes. There are frequent references to Joan's physical scars and crippled foot, the result of an accident in Brooklyn; and these references are symbolically important. Maud, who has been spared the traumas Joan experienced abroad, is herself emotionally crippled by years of 'stiff regimentation'. Her life is of a piece with the 'solid yellow square' of chrysanthemums which Joan finds 'distasteful' and 'sinister'. Maud's sterile respectability and stolidity are suggested in Collymore's image of her face 'framed within [the] circumambience of chrysanthemums'; and the grave she has chosen for Joan and herself – 'a neat square of trimly mown grass . . . enclosed by an elegant wrought-iron fence' – reminds one of her square, stiffly regimented garden. Collymore implies that Maud's antiseptic life and her formally organised landscape are complementary: like her perfectly arranged, perfectly cultivated flowers, she too is a credit to her neighbourhood. Maud, furthermore, has always managed to do the right thing: she met and married the right man at the right time; and he conveniently died at the right time, 'leaving her quite well off'. For all its respectability and material comforts, Maud's life has not been fulfilling; but Joan's unconventional existence, which Maud abjures, has brought her a happiness Maud seems never to have experienced. When Joan tries to tell of her life abroad, Maud refuses to listen, as if her rejection of her sister's life has been compromised by a subconscious desire and envy. Maud's continual preachiness comes, one feels, from her 'self-righteousness and a complete lack of sensibility'.

Collymore's use of contrast is a notable feature of his short fiction. In at least two stories, 'Some People Are Meant to Live

Alone' and 'Miss Edison', he uses setting in a contrasting mode in order to reinforce or enhance character or theme. In the former story Uncle Arthur's 'gaunt and cockeyed' house matches the owner's distorted withdrawal and brooding alienation. Like Jones, his fictional alter ego, Uncle Arthur has 'come to terms with . . . the essential loneliness of humanity'. The young narrator, who has listened with fascination to his uncle's story, is not only receptive to Uncle Arthur's alienation, he also discovers that he shares the older man's brooding sensibilities and his uncommon attraction for solitariness. In 'Miss Edison' Collymore makes several references to the sedative landscape of cloud-flecked sky, swaying cabbage-palms, 'a green garden-seat in the shade of the hibiscus border' and the 'bougainvillaea-shaded verandah'. These descriptions, which may appear mere gratuitous colour, reinforce the contrast between the compelling beauty of the mental hospital's landscape and the dark reality of the lost, blighted lives within its forbidding walls. Miss Edison's maniacal laughter at the end of the story is all the more chilling because of its juxtaposition with the serene environment to whose soothing rhythms the narrator had yielded.

In 'To Meet Her Mother' and 'The Diaries' contrast is the hub around which an important issue turns. In the former a youngster's discovery of painful reality is placed within the context of a universal archetype. Collymore sets up a contrast between the dreaming, love-smitten youngster and the ugly reality from which he tries to escape. The fat, strident Barbadian women on the bus are the antithesis of his vision of ideal femininity, an ideal embodied in Sylphide, the euphoniously named girl with whom he is in love. When he is confronted with Sylphide's obese mother, the dramatic and arresting contrast between grotesque reality and her photograph as a young woman is too overwhelming for him, since Sylphide is a facsimile of her mother's photograph and the young lover can see the future writ large. This time he is forced to flee another reality, that of his own shallowness. The dreaming boy, Collymore implies, pays a high price when dream is contaminated by reality. In 'The Diaries' – one of Collymore's most carefully controlled narratives – the lawyer's fascination with the bizarre events of Selina Casper's life, which he deciphers from her disintegrating diaries, stems not so much from his discovery of the events themselves, but from the contrast between these events and Selina's coldness and respectability, both successfully cultivated over several years. The lawyer is astonished at the remarkable variety of human beings: Selina's diaries are a revelation of that dark underside that suddenly surfaces in the most surprising of places. 'The Diaries' also illustrates one of Collymore's strengths as a short-story writer: vivid characterisation. In many fine short stories what the writer leaves unsaid is often as important as what is said. If this is regarded as a criterion of good short-story writing, then 'The Diaries' is one of Collymore's best efforts. The sparseness of the narrative is admirable, and Collymore's use of the first-person point of view is sure and engaging. The narrator, the executor of Selina Casper's will, reveals little of himself; yet one comes to know him through his astute, slightly ironic comments and observations of Selina Casper whose dark and secret character emerges as he reads her trenchant diaries. His staid tone suggests that he is circumspect, not given to easy condemnation of human follies, wry, perceptive and disarmingly ironic.

The first-person point of view is also successful in 'The Man Who Loved Attending Funerals'. This story also has some of Poe's resonances, but the narrative voice has Collymore's ironic notes. Collymore shows that his narrator's preoccupation with death and funerals, and above all with the social rituals of death, is not simply an eccentricity, but an avocation, indeed the only passion of which he is capable. One's attention is drawn to the narrator's egotism and smugness as well as the emphasis he gives to proper form, style and the superficial proprieties associated with social rituals. He does not use his gift of foretelling death in order to warn and commiserate with those who need it; nor does the gift deepen his understanding of the mystery of death. Only his self-conception is enhanced, his sense of personal exaltation. He even suspects that somehow he has been apotheosised. Having failed in virtually all endeavours – particularly in human relations – he devotes all of his energies to what is ultimately a denial of love. He discovers, and it is not a particularly disconcerting discovery for him, that friends may perhaps see his own imminent death as he saw the death of others, as a vindication of their own survival. At the end Collymore reinforces the narrator's invincible shallowness: he hopes, indeed expects, that all of the required proprieties shall be maintained at his own funeral.

In 'The Tragic Circumstances Surrounding the Death of Angela Westmore' – the ironic title sets the tone for the rest of the story – the focus of Collymore's interest is Guff, the 'accomplished bore' whose eccentricity and implacable dullness push his listeners' patience to the limits. But Collymore is also interested in Guff's two harassed listeners. Again description, explanation and other authorial interruptions are carefully controlled, and the ironic, sometimes sarcastic, tone and diction of the narrative voice adequately convey both characterisation and the burden of having to tolerate a man of Guff's oppressive boorishness. Here are the story's opening paragraphs:

> It was only this morning that I learnt that Guff and his family had left the island.
>
> I read the brief announcement twice to make sure, and hurried to communicate the news to Phil. He paused in his shaving, closed his eyes, and murmured, 'Thank God.' And Phil isn't what one would call a religious man.

The rest of the story, which is a successful reproduction of Guff's tediousness, is an explanation of Phil's trite but, under the circumstances, eloquent expression of relief. The admirable forbearance of Guff's listeners is also conveyed in their attitude: they do not detest Guff, however pressed they are to do so; instead, Guff at once repels and fascinates them as an oddity, a phenomenon who has transformed boorishness into an art. At the end of his account of Angela Westmore's death by drowning, they watch Guff's departure in silence, a 'silence', Collymore writes, 'tempered with something that was almost awe'.

Laureston Baker, the central character of 'Mr Baker Forgets Himself', is 'enclosed within the impervious walls of self', and this egocentricity turns him into a thoroughly rebarbative individual. His inflated ego, however, is deflated when he is struck down by a potent strain of influenza, and he subsequently comes to recognise the frailty of his own body and his very existence in the universal order of things. His generous, selfless act of rescuing a stricken kitten from the rain (under different circumstances he would have given the animal short shrift) and then taking the kitten into his sickbed is an affirmation of his oneness with all things, even the least significant, the most dispensable of things. Mr Baker's frailty matches the kitten's, and there are redemptive resonances in his death from pneumonia shortly after he rescues the animal. The old man of 'There's Always the Angels' is another carefully drawn character. At the centre of the story is the old man's painful recognition of the Virgilian *lacrimae rerum*. It is worth noting that the story was published in February 1945, by which time the world had supped full with the horrors of the War. The bleakness of the story might well owe something to these horrors. Even though he imaginatively recreates what he conceives of as a perfect universe, something goes wrong, as indeed it did in the original creation: it is as if the loss of the Edenic dream is both necessary and inevitable.

Collymore's skill in character delineation is not confined to adults. In 'The Snag' seven-year-old Mark's idyll at Graham Lodge is shattered by the appearance of the old woman Miss Martha. His sojourn in the countryside is probably the fantasy of all boys; but his pleasures are counteracted and then severely undermined by the arrival of Miss Martha who is in a state of physical decay which Mark finds revolting. But Mark is a sensitive, imaginative and perceptive youngster, which Collymore conveys by maintaining a discreet distance between the narrative voice and Mark's observing sensibilities. Mark comes to understand the inevitability of time's ravages. Unlike stories such as 'Proof' and 'Second Attempt', the ending of 'The Snag' is not contrived. The snag in Mark's happy sojourn at Graham Lodge is the shocking reality of Miss Martha's dereliction and his unmistakable realisation that to this favour we must all come. The Mark persona reappears in two other stories. In 'Mark Learns Another Lesson' the observing boy is allowed to reflect and comment as a nine-year-old would. The youngster has a keen and witty eye for detail; unable to find the exact word to describe the fascinating Miss Vi Driscoll, he gives us this vivid picture:

> There she sat in a very large chair and yet there were parts of her protruding all around. Her face was set amid a vast expanse of wattle-like folds and chins, and when she sighed the lower part of her face was completely obscured by a tremendous upheaval of bosom. She reminded him of nothing so much as a picture he'd seen once of a captive balloon, imperfectly blown out and wabbly. 'Enor-mious,' thought Mark.

Mark is sensitive to nuances that might escape other nine-year-old boys, and his sensibilities force him to see, and then express, the unfairness of God in the Jacob and Esau story. For this he pays a price: his teachers accuse him of blasphemy, and he is threatened with hell. It is the first stage in the loss of his innocence. In 'A Day at the Races', Collymore's last published story, Mark undergoes a sort of *rite de passage* when, contrary to the wishes of his staid aunts at Graham Lodge, he goes to the races at Garrison Savannah. The world of thoroughbred racing in the West Indies is fiercely masculine; and when the boy successfully fends for himself in this unknown world – he even holds the stakes for two gamblers, hears cursing, witnesses arguments and a fight – it is his first intimate experience of this uncompromising male world.

Collymore's short stories are not without their weaknesses. He has a tendency, for instance, to adhere too fastidiously to the nineteenth-century concept of the 'well-made story'. In the December 1943 number of *Bim* 'One of the Editors' explains what the magazine requires of its short stories:

> These should be well told in reasonably good English with at least a semblance of a plot, sustained interest and something of a climax. Do not write merely to express yourself or to mend the world or to elevate humanity. Give us something with a wide appeal – and a love interest is always welcome.[3]

None of these recommendations is unworthy of short fiction; but together they amount to a formula-type story. Some of Collymore's plots tend to follow an almost classical line of exposition, rising action, climax and unambiguous resolution. Of these, the last feature is perhaps his most noticeable defect. 'Proof' (1942), the first of his published stories, is a good example. The plot is melodramatic: the innocent Tamara, who has been unjustly accused of espionage, is living with her husband and infant in daily dread of arrest and punishment; driven to desperation, they decide to commit suicide. The terror and suspense which paralyse them are effectively called up, but the tragic ending to which everything has been building is suddenly and unexpectedly averted at the eleventh hour by a contrived peripeteia. 'Twin-Ending' and 'Second Attempt' are also marred by defective endings. In the former Collymore gives the reader two endings: the happy one, or the semi-tragic. Neither is satisfactory. The first – a tragic end to a nasty love triangle is averted when it is discovered that there has been a misunderstanding – is another example of the sudden reversal; and the second – one twin has betrayed her sister's trust – is too predictable to be effective.

Collymore's weaknesses, however, are largely compensated for by his effective use of language. His descriptive language, which is as controlled as his plots, is never gratuitous. Even in 'Proof', which is not one of his best efforts, Collymore uses the bleakness of November in Leningrad to convey the bleakness within the hearts of his characters. The walk taken by the frightened family through the ominous streets with their threatening buildings and searching faces enhances the story's tone of impending disaster:

> That day they went for a walk, the three of them. Dark and grey the huge buildings towered above the snowy streets. They walked past the shop windows. To her it was all terrible. Every face that looked at them might be the one. Every now and then she would glance over her shoulder. Surely they were being followed.

In other stories, 'The Diaries' for example, the sparseness of the narrative achieves an excellent intensity of focus. Immediacy of impact is also noticeable in stories such as 'The Man Who Loved Attending Funerals', 'Rewards and Chrysanthemums' and 'Shadows'. In 'Rewards and Chrysanthemums' the sisters' incompatibility, subtly suggested in their stiff but not unloving relationship, the vastness of the barrier that has separated them – all of this is forcefully brought home to the reader in the final scene of the story:

> She grabbed Joan's arm and tugged her along. 'Come quick, quick. We must, we must. Your Christmas present.'
>
> Completely ignoring the increasing volume of the shower, she continued to drag her sister across the slippery pathway to the other end of the churchyard where a neat square of trimly mown grass lay enclosed by an elegant wrought-iron fence.
>
> Maud halted before it and pointed to it proudly. 'There!' she announced.
>
> 'But what . . . what . . . whose . . . ?'
>
> Maud placed her arm around Joan and squeezed her affectionately. Her face was alight with sisterly devotion, and her eyes, behind the spectacles dimmed with raindrops, brimmed over with more than joy.
>
> 'It's for *us*, dear, it's for you and I when we pass on.' She paused to sneeze. 'There now, my darling, aren't you delighted?'

Collymore also writes effective dialogue. In stories such as 'Some People Are Meant to Live Alone' the dialogue is neither contrived nor artificial: it emerges naturally from the situations and seems appropriate for the speaker. Instead of conveying Bill Church's shock through conventional description, Collymore achieves a more forceful effect by emphasising Uncle Arthur's chillingly calm tone as he tells the story of his crime. It is as if Arthur has destroyed a pest, and now the comfortable tenor of his life can continue untrammelled.

Frank Collymore died in 1980, and during his lifetime he was much honoured for his invaluable service to the growth of West Indian fiction. Had it not been for his perseverance *Bim* might not have survived, a disaster, surely, for West Indian literature. 'To look through the fifty-five numbers of *Bim* to date [1973],' Edward Baugh says, 'is to see the history of West Indian literature during the last thirty years.'[4] Baugh places Collymore at the centre of the West Indian literary awakening of the 1940s: 'The contacts with writers which he made through the magazine enabled his influence to work at a very direct personal level and gave scope to the generosity of spirit and capacity for friendship which are among his chief virtues.'[5] After 1971 Collymore's eyes began to deteriorate and he published no more stories. His work as editor of *Bim* under dire financial circumstances assures him a permanent place in the history of West Indian literature. Here is George Lamming's assessment of *Bim*'s importance:

> There are not many West Indian writers today who did not use *Bim* as a kind of platform, the surest, if not the only avenue, by which they might reach a literate and sensitive reading public, and almost all of the West Indians who are now writers in a more professional sense and whose work has compelled the attention of readers and writers in other countries, were introduced, so to speak, by *Bim*.[6]

Edward Baugh has suggested that 'one of *Bim*'s achievements is that it encouraged the development of the short story form as a significant medium for the West Indian literary imagination'.[7] In time Collymore's short stories will surely be regarded as an important contribution to that development.

Harold Barratt

Notes

1 See *An Index to Bim: 1942–1972*, ed Reinhard Sander (Trinidad and Tobago: UWI Extra-Mural Studies Unit, 1973), for a complete listing of Collymore's short stories.
2 Edward Baugh, 'Introduction', *An Index to Bim*, p 11.
3 'What *Bim* Requires', *Bim*, Vol 1, No 3 (December, 1943), 76.
4 Baugh, 'Introduction', *An Index to Bim*, p 9.
5 Baugh, 'Frank Collymore: A Biographical Portrait', *Savacou*, 7/8 (January–June, 1973), 145.
6 Quoted by Baugh, 'Frank Collymore', *Fifty Caribbean Writers: A Bio-Bibliographical Critical Sourcebook*, ed Daryl Dance (New York: Greenwood Press, 1986), p 123.
7 Ibid, p 124.

Select Bibliography

Baugh, Edward. 'Frank Collymore: A Biographical Portrait'. *Savacou*, 7/8 (January-June, 1973), 139–148;

'Frank Collymore'. *Fifty Caribbean Writers: A Bio-Bibliographical Critical Sourcebook*. Ed. Daryl Dance. New York: Greenwood Press, 1986, pp 122–132;

'Introduction'. *An Index to Bim: 1942–1972*. Ed. Reinhard Sander. Trinidad and Tobago: UWI Extra-Mural Studies Unit, 1973, pp 7–17.

Collymore, Frank. 'An Evening with the Poets'. *Bim*, Vol 2, No 5 (February, 1945), 33–35, 67–88;

'Impressions of a Tour'. *Bim*, Vol 3, No 9 (December, 1948), 66–74; Vol 3, No 10 (June, 1949), 162-170;

'An Introduction to the Poetry of Derek Walcott'. *Bim*, Vol 3, No 10 (June, 1949), 125–132;

'Non Immemor: Reminiscences of Frank Collymore'. *Bim*, Vol 15, No 57 (March, 1974), 3–15; Vol 15, No 58 (June, 1975), 79–86;

Notes for a Glossary of Words and Phrases of Barbadian Dialect. 1955; 4th ed. Barbados: Advocate, 1970;

'The Story of *Bim*'. *Bim*, Vol 10, No 38 (January–June, 1964), 68–72;

'Writing in the West Indies: A Survey'. *Tamarack Review*, No 14 (1960), 111–124.

Sander, Reinhard, and Ian Munro. 'Chatting About Bim: Excerpts from a Conversation with Frank Collymore'. *An Index to Bim: 1942-1972*. Trinidad and Tobago: UWI Extra-Mural Studies Unit, 1973, pp 18–23.

Wickham, John. 'Colly: A Profile'. *The Bajan and South Caribbean*, January, 1973, pp 12, 14, 16–19, 31.